THE BRIDE, THE GROOM, AND THE GHOST

"The bride roams around invisibly, the groom feels invisible, and the ghost is the only one who is visible."

Ann Marie Ruby

Disclaimer:

This book ("*The Bride, The Groom, And The Ghost*") in no way
represents or endorses any religious, philosophical, political, or
scientific view. It has been written in good faith for people of all
cultures and beliefs. This book has been written in American English.
There may be minor variations in spelling and dates due to translations
or minor discrepancies in historical records.

This is a work of fiction. Names, characters, places, and incidents are
the product of the author's imagination or are used fictitiously. Any
resemblance to actual persons, living or dead, is purely coincidental.
While the cities, towns, and villages are real, references to historical
events, real people, or real locations are used fictitiously.

Published in the United States of America, 2024.

ISBN-13: 979-8-9875085-8-9

DEDICATION

"Elders are respected as the experienced and all knowledgeable, yet as they stand next to you the young with no experience, it is then their experience through life or your inexperience both are criticized without fair evaluation."

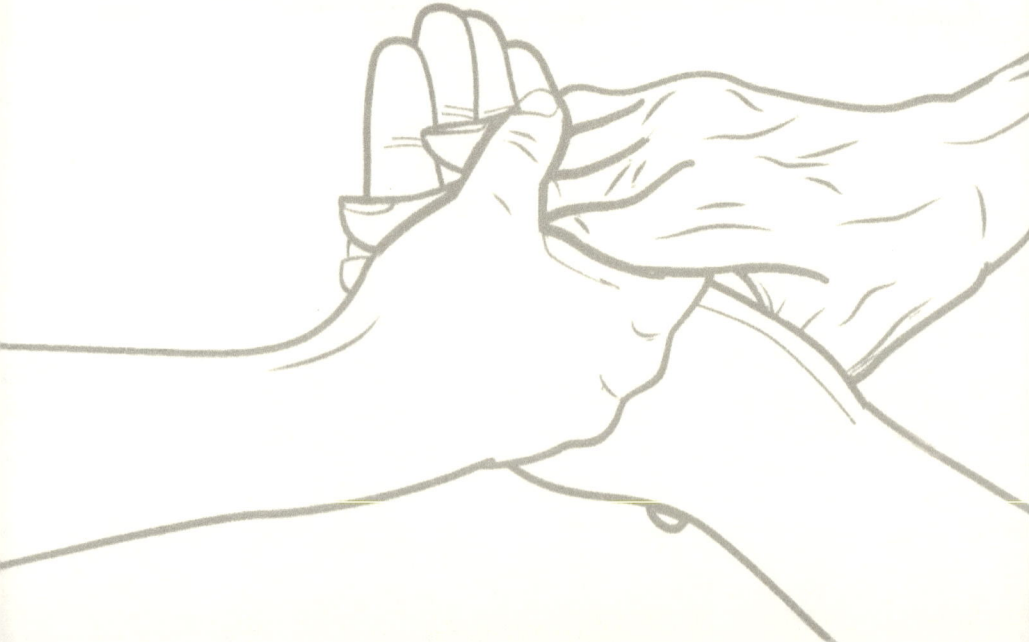

Dedication is a gift from the dedicant to the dedicated. This book was written to raise awareness of a hidden yet very widely recognized humanitarian crisis, discrimination. There are so many laws of the land that protect humans against any form of discrimination. Yet why do we still in the twenty-first century hear of so many acts of discrimination taking place all around us?

Some of these acts include racial, religious, ethnic, medical, disability, sexual, status as a parent, pregnancy, and age discrimination. No one should be subjected to such cruel treatments. Be the human, not the demon. All of you suffering from any discriminatory actions, may you find your voice against all discrimination.

In this book, I have brought up the elderly people who are members of our society. They, however, feel like the neglected part of society. Today, medical science has gifted the elderly people another chance at life. People are living longer, and this magical gift should be celebrated, not treated as a burden.

Marrying later in life or just enjoying a better and healthier life has become a normal part of this generation as people are living longer. The retirement age, however, remains the same. Perceptions of the perceivers are also a huge factor in this humanitarian crisis.

In 1969, Robert Neil Butler, the founding director of the National Institute on Aging, had spoken about age-related discrimination. The term ageism was originally used to describe discrimination against elderly people. Ageism, however, is now also used to describe prejudice against teenage or younger people.

Shockingly, one in two people are ageist against the elderly population of the world. These discriminatory behaviors are found at the workplace, in healthcare systems, and all around the society. No one realizes how this will affect our own senior citizens for they will suffer psychologically and emotionally all alone as the victims of our treatment. We are all guilty through our actions toward the aging population. Sometimes, we do it knowingly and a lot of times, unknowingly. Yet we all do it.

We leave our elderly people alone to give them some privacy, but some are just left behind out of negligence. Some are just ignored as if they don't even belong in the society. In the workforce, the young and the fit have not given them a second chance. Everyone seems to forget the path of life is a one-way road.

How could we the society forget the world health crisis, for today health issues are not limited to medical insurance and medical bills, but medical and disability

iv

discrimination. We can't forget the immunocompromised people as they are always being criticized or seen differently. Here, we the young, the healthy, the immunocompromised, and the elderly all walk toward the same ending.

The elderly are expected to reach first as they began the journey first. Some immunocompromised people reach faster, even though in this race, the winner is not who goes there first but who goes there last. You the young and healthy will end up at the same spot in a few years. Today, if you feel neglected as a teenager then you probably will understand tomorrow when you will be the elderly and again feel neglected. So today, let's awaken through our inner hearts and say no to our own discriminatory behaviors.

This fictional paranormal novel investigates this humanitarian crisis through a paranormal gothic thriller. Here I want all of you to hold on to the hands of my two leading characters and a special person who will take your hearts away. I know three is always a crowd in most novels, but believe me, it is not in this novel. I want you all to see the world through their eyes. The love birds in this story started their journey as youngsters who faced racial discrimination in their youth. Now as the elderly, they have landed upon a path we all will only be at soon.

You will find reincarnation, ghosts, spirits, murders, and paranormal gothic events take place. In this novel, you will be a witness to a murder mystery that happened over a hundred years ago in the previous incarnation. This mystery, however, we must solve in this new reincarnated life. Join me in this magical world where I control the fate. Here I bring in my paranormal helping hands from my *Kasteel Vrederic* series.

New Orleans, a city in Louisiana, sits by the Mississippi River which flows into the Gulf of Mexico. This city is nicknamed "The Big Easy" and is known as a melting pot of French, American, and African cultures combined. This is where I have set my story *The Bride, The Groom, And The Ghost*.

I want the world to be acquainted with this amazing place as I loved living in this city. Come along with this book and get to know why this city is loved by so many across the globe. Here people are resilient as they taught the world how to rebuild a city when Mother Nature had struck them through one of the worst storms in history known as Hurricane Katrina.

The citizens of "The Big Easy" teach all to never give up on hope as hope never gives up on us. When you do eventually get a chance to visit this remarkable city, keep your eyes open. Just maybe, you too will see the bride, the groom, and the ghost as you join the city during its late-winter Mardi Gras parades.

This book is written through three sets of eyes as within all stories, there are different sides to the same story. This story is complete through three diaries. So, we first see through the eyes of a young ghost bride who faced sexual discrimination. She remains ever young for she had left this Earth as a victim of discrimination.

Even after taking her last breath, she is trying to help her elderly beloved who is now facing ageism. The cold frosted hands come breaking the barriers of death as she tries to guide the old, withered hands. Who says there are no helping hands left on Earth? If not above the ground, then maybe from beneath the ground someone will be able to help.

In the second diary, you will see through the eyes of a retired groom who tries to bridge the difference of the paranormal and reality within a gothic love story. The third diary is the conclusion told through the eyes of the ghost who was a victim of age and medical discrimination. He teaches all that any kind of discrimination should not be accepted. Sometimes it takes a ghost through his life story to get the attention of our society.

This paranormal gothic thriller is written to remind all discriminating individuals to fear karma. You the discriminators were committing the acts from your hiding spots, so no one knew who you were. Today with open social media, you are caught in the act. Yet today I see the discriminators too are not afraid to commit these horrific acts. This book will be a powerful reminder, even if you forget your horrific actions time and tide will not forget or forgive.

May this book guide all to live together peacefully with one another, not against one another. May the world citizens all awaken like a magical phoenix and accept all race, color, and religion into one home where we accept all ages, respect the elders, and don't ignore the young ones. I hope this book teaches all to be understanding and compassionate about the person standing next to you even if you don't like them.

This book I dedicate to all individuals and their family members who have unjustly suffered under any discriminatory acts.

AGEISM IS A CULTURAL ILLNESS

I, the traveler of life,

Walked through my life

To be the wise.

Yet where I stand,

I know I have

Much more steps to go,

Before I become the wise.

Yet I watch new travelers,

Walking toward me,

Calling me ancient.

I wonder, when did I

Become the old,

As I have so much more

Path to cover,

And so much more to do.

I wonder why you,

The new traveler,

Not far behind me,

Are so fearful to be

At the same place,

I so gracefully stand.

I realize you are not

Afraid of death.

Yet it seems you

Fear to be at the same corner,

I so sophisticatedly stand.

I know I have with me

Knowledge and wisdom,

Yet I still am traveling,

To be the wise.

Why do I see

So many travelers

Look terribly hostile,

For it seems they don't want

To move on forward,

And be where I am standing,

For they fear not the path,

Not the journey,

Nor do they fear death,

Yet they fear where I stand.

How do I teach this society,

Not to fear me,

Nor fear where I stand?

For I know you too shall

Be here soon.

Then you will see

That others are taking the same journey,

THE BRIDE, THE GROOM, AND THE GHOST

Not far behind you,

Yet as you have

Taught them well,

They too shall

Fear even you.

Let me the wise

Share with you

Lessons from where I stand

As I am not ill, and

Neither will you be

When you too stand where I

Am standing,

Yet at your own time.

A word from

I, the wise,

Shall be passed on to you,

Before it is too late,

As the people

You have taught today

Will tomorrow

From your given lessons

Be frightened of you.

So today,

Do tell the society,

This message was given to you

By a previous traveler,

Who had said,

Ageism is not an illness,

Yet within this society,

AGEISM IS A CULTURAL ILLNESS.

TABLE OF CONTENTS

THE BRIDE:

First Diary

"I became the bride yet never the wife as I roamed around as a ghost bride."

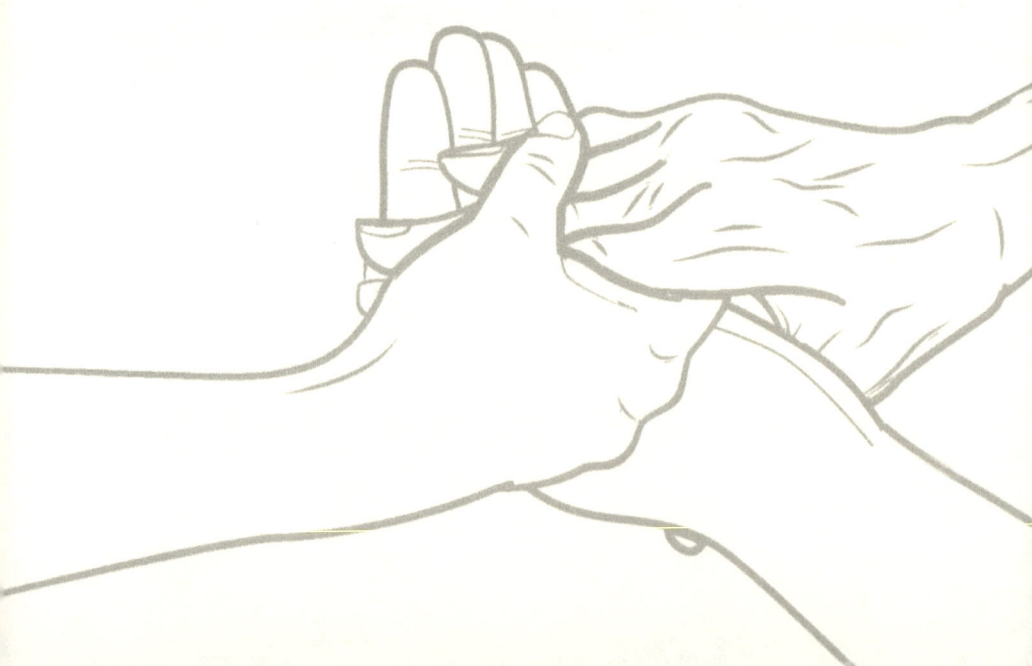

PROLOGUE:

The Ghost Bride Of New Orleans

"The bridge of life and death separates me from my beloved while I roam around the streets of New Orleans as a ghost bride."

The lightning from the skies touched the ground as thunder roared after her, warning a war is about to brew on Earth. I watch Mother Nature and her different forms as I know she is always trying to guide us. Take notes from nature, as nature's warnings should never be ignored.

Remember even though time passes by, Mother Nature's guidance and forewarning remain the same. Do you forget lessons of the past or do you keep them in your chest as a guidance from the past? The past is a teacher as is the present and so shall be the future. All the teachers converse about their guidance through our footsteps.

On a very stormy night, I walked through the crowded streets of New Orleans, Louisiana. This state has so many pages of itself stored within the history books. On April 30, 1812, Louisiana was declared the 18th state of the United States. The US had purchased Louisiana from France in 1803 after the French emperor Napoleon Bonaparte lost interest in establishing an empire in North America. France was in a war against the British and needed the money.

I don't need money nor food as I am a lonely stranger. Neither the rain nor the frigid weather touch me. They are all there but are very invisible to me. Or I wonder, am I invisible to them? The memories and the past are not invisible, nor could they be erased.

I can never forget the massacre of 1866 as you too must have read all about it as this was written within the pages of your history books. Maybe you know it as the New Orleans Massacre when black men were attacked and murdered by white rioters. These were the defeated soldiers who belonged to the Confederate States of America during President Andrew Jackson's time.

I was a privileged white woman who was madly in love with my beloved husband, after the US Constitution abolished slavery in 1864. We allowed ourselves to finally be with one another. My husband was a freed black man who was granted full rights as a citizen. We were blessed with happiness as my beloved was free and could be his own person. For now, he was not owned by anyone like as if he was an animal not a human being. We secretly wed and had been at the wrong place at the wrong time.

As I walked through the famous Bourbon Street in New Orleans in the twentieth century, I saw the decorated streetlights and the loud musical instruments playing the sweet and sorrow songs calling the lovers to go wild just this one night. I could smell freshly cooked gumbo, jambalaya, red beans, and rice. I watched people carry fresh baked beignets and realized how I miss being home.

Café Du Monde, a coffee stand which stood here in the French Market in 1862, a few years before I passed away, still was standing there. They were still making their famous beignets. The owners must have changed through time but a family strong with their bond through generations still have kept up their business. I wished I too had a family so my children and grandchildren could have written my life story throughout time. Instead, I saw strangers who were walking the roads I had once traveled upon in another time.

Maybe they could see the ghost bride, dressed all in white with a century-old dried flowers, still roaming the streets of New Orleans. The smell of familiar food and familiar music called my inner soul. I wished I could taste this food one more time. The nocturnal street was buzzing with tourists from around the globe. I followed a very famous familiar businessman who was still in his late twenties flirting with all the women he could get his hands on. Born with a silver spoon, he was handed down a huge business empire by his rich father.

He wouldn't remember me, the woman he had tried to rape during the New Orleans Massacre in 1866. I watched him with agony, pain, and fury. I wanted to harm him so bad, but I controlled my temper as what else could a ghost do? Maybe an evil person becomes an evil ghost and good people become good ghosts. Today, I am the feared ghost, yet it was just a while ago I died fearing them.

I watched the famous businessman who owned cruise ships around the country cheat on his newlywed wife in 1866. When my newlywed husband and I jumped on his ship to get away from our family, this monster had come after us. He was a newlywed man going on a honeymoon. As he was not satisfied with just one woman, his corrupt eyes had fallen on me.

My parents cursed me to Hell for running away with a black man. Little did they know, I would be living in Hell as today I am a ghost bride who can't even ask anyone for help or forgiveness. If I could still marry anyone, I would only marry my beloved in every lifetime as a human or as a ghost bride. My beloved's family too had cursed him with hardship throughout his life.

His mother cursed him, "May you always be lonely and never find a wife or happiness in your life. May your bride die and leave you alone to rot all by yourself. You have disgraced us by running away with the daughter of the man who gave us freedom. He stood by us and today you put us to shame. Go away from here and know my curse will follow you to wherever you go or wherever you may land."

I watched his mother as she was my caretaker and had so lovingly taken care of me from childhood. Without any thought, she had just cursed me to death and her only son to a life of misery. If she only knew she had cursed her son and me throughout our reincarnations too, I wonder would she still curse him or take it back?

I was a newlywed bride going on a honeymoon with my husband. We promised to wait to unite until our wedding night as we were both churchgoers and God-fearing. We sat and talked under the stars as we promised to be one another's eternally. I never knew I had to wed a white man and was forbidden to marry a black man. I had cried for over a hundred years. I don't know which year it is now.

I remember how my beloved and I had run toward the cruise ship we were promised to be given a ride on. The riots broke out and my family members who had freed their own workers were hunting them down in the same crowd. I asked my brother to not get involved and let them be free.

My brother Andrew Froster stamped his foot and shouted in fury, "No, I won't leave them alone! I will walk with my people and slaughter all of them today!"

I told him, "Then, slaughter me first because that's how you will get my husband."

It was then the rich businessman, Mr. Drake Crow, came and became our saving grace. He took us under his protection and hid us in his ship. It was dark at night when I watched Mr. Crow, a white man in his late fifties with his newlywed wife who was in her twenties get aboard the ship.

That night, my husband and I were both happy. We thought it was our wedding night when we would make love on the boat under the stars in our own cabin. Free from land and all the riots, we would have our eternal love story written through our union. I would be touched and loved by my lawfully wedded husband.

All my dreams would come true tonight. I had stolen some kisses from my husband, yet we promised to be virgins until our wedding night. Unbeknownst to us, it was not in our fate. As I heard my beloved's mother's curses over our heads, I saw the very drunken businessman come into our room.

Mr. Crow smirked and laughed as he whispered, "I just raped the woman you saw had come with me. She was a twenty-year-old virgin. She is not my wife, nor will she ever be as I have a family. You see, my old wife and I have five children and she does not have any idea about my affairs, nor does she care as long as I provide for her."

He tried to hold me down and take off my clothes. I scratched his hands with my nails and thought I would bite him and leave him bleeding. He saw a pretty woman dressed as a bride, not a woman dressed in rage who would do anything to save her honor.

Mr. Crow the demon screamed, shouted, and yelled in pain from my scratches, "So now I want to rape you! You young man can just go outside and pretend you did not see anything. I will pay you for all the things your heart desires. A new home and money to start a business. Now, just walk outside for a few minutes. I want to have your virgin bride first. I will be done soon, then she can be all yours."

My beloved said to our savior, now our predator, "Over my dead body. For as long as I breathe, you will never touch my wife. I know I will spend the rest of my life in jail as no one will ever listen to the true facts of a black man. All shall believe your words, but I don't care. I will protect my wedded wife at any cost. If I breathe, you shall never lay a finger on her."

My married life was very short-lived. All my dreams just evaporated into thin air. In front of me, my beloved was shot and thrown out to the bottom of the cold Mississippi

River. Then, I saw the monster come toward me like nothing happened. He stood and just laughed and screamed like a mad animal. His shrieks and breathing became hysterical as if he was high on something. He jumped up and down like a creature, not a human.

I heard my beloved's last words still linger in the air, "Beloved of mine, promise to be mine not in just one lifetime but over and over again. Until we unite, I will be reborn life after life only for you. Do recognize me if I change my form. My darling, know I love you eternally. I only pray my name remains the same, so you do recognize me. I will forever be your Silas Coleridge Vivour."

I witnessed my life end in front of me as the monster shrieked, "You are still young and naïve as you wanted to marry a black man. You see at your age, you can't decide for yourself. You are young and brainless, so let me show you a real man and how it's done properly. Just have sex with me and then you will be free. All young women and little girls dress up and put on makeup like they all want to be a bride, so why not be a one night's bride? Then, you will be free."

I saw the monster was screaming and had completely gone out of control. The man who had helped a free black man had taken off his good man face and showed his real face. He was a living and breathing dragon who was on fire and cared not for anyone on his path. His rage would burn everything around him. The dragon watched me with his ugly face. The saliva from his mouth dripped all around his lips and drained down his chin.

He then said, "I like them young and even if she is a child, I don't care. Young people are always lost and stranded, so let me take you in as my mistress. When you become my age, you will find your own path. I have taken so many young girls and made them into complete women."

The monster killed my husband, then he put down all young people and called all women prostitutes who were ready to go to bed with the rich and famous at their will. He was proudly talking about children and how he cared not even if the person he desired for the night was a young girl or a woman. He was a demon in human form who believed young people don't have the knowledge to know the difference between good and evil.

I told him, "Never will I allow you or anyone to touch me as my beloved is still alive. Sex to you is hunger and lust. You catch with force and money. In my eyes, it's only between twin flames. My husband is a good swimmer, and he will survive your bullets. He will come for me."

The monster came and tried to take off my wedding gown. I knew my wedding gown was sacred and he couldn't touch it.

I screamed, "Don't touch me or I will take my own life before you can touch me! Like I told you, I am a married woman! I belong only to my husband Silas."

His mistress came in and laughed and made fun of me, saying, "It's all right. We all say that at the beginning, then we just enjoy the ride. You'll get used to it. You can call it rape or forced sex or consensual. It's all going to be the same in the bazaar of prostitutes. We get raped, have forced sex, or at times just go along with it. You can be a bride for the night. Just imagine you're having sex with your beloved Silas."

On a silver platter with fresh apples, I saw there was a knife to cut the apples. I picked up the knife and pointed it to my own chest. I knew the platter was decorated for my wedding night.

The monster laughed, "You are a churchgoer. You won't commit suicide, will you? It's against your belief."

I asked my Lord for guidance as I did believe suicide was against my belief yet how could I live knowing on my wedding night I was raped by the murderer of my husband? I saw my whole life flash before me. My prayers and my devotion to the one and only man, my husband, was now only a dream.

The demon man came closer. He was completely naked and walked slowly toward me. His mistress stood there without even trying to give me a saving hand of grace. A woman was just watching another woman about to be raped and did nothing. She walked away without being my friend in need.

I prayed, "My Lord, I choose death over being raped by the murderer of my husband. I have prayed for your intercession, but I have no one who can help me. Whatever punishment you have stored for me, I will endure. How could going to my own Lord and asking my Creator to forgive me be worse than being alive without the love of my life in the hands of a rapist and a murderer?"

I tried to save my life as I believed I might just live after my jump into the cold river. As I held on to the knife threatening all if they would come near me, I didn't hesitate to do what I had to do. I recited The Lord's Prayer and Hail Mary. I said Glory Be and recited an Act of Contrition. As I said, "In the Name of the Father, and of the Son, and of the Holy Spirit, Amen," I jumped into the cold Mississippi River.

This river today runs through ten states and drains into over thirty states. It finally falls into the Gulf of Mexico. I prayed the great river could protect an innocent woman from the hands of a dragon that chased me. As a Catholic, I tried to do the right thing and didn't support this act.

I asked my Lord, "How could I give away the only thing that I promised, and you my Lord too have said to save for only my husband?"

I thought I could maybe swim away from the monster as the tides were not high. Then, I could find my husband. While the monster held on to my hands, I cut his hands and mine. I let go of all the last hope of my living life.

I remembered only then as I said, "Oh my Lord, but I never learned to swim. Silas help, I never learned to swim."

I tried searching for my beloved as I screamed and told him, "I love you eternally Silas. May I be yours in every life and may you be mine in all our reincarnated lives. I shall be only yours in life and in death. Be mine eternally my beloved as this beloved will live or die with your name upon my lips."

I repeated the phrase until everything was becoming dark and I could see nothing. I still whispered for the world above and beyond to hear and witness a beloved's last words.

I screamed for the world to hear me, yet my words came out as whispers, "I love you Silas Coleridge Vivour! Forever I am yours. My Lord, I tried to swim and save my life and honor, but I just can't figure out how to."

I drowned, or some of you will say I took my own life. I ask you is it a sin to go after my husband and try to save him even if that meant I would die? Is death not more loving than being the mistress of a monster? I tried to search for my husband when I woke up. I don't know when or for how long I was roaming the streets of New Orleans, not realizing I was a ghost bride. How could I still be here in the same clothing if no one could see or hear me?

The days and the years passed yet I realized I was being punished by the curses of my own mother and mother-in-law. The two mothers who should have blessed me had cursed me even in death. I wish this Earth could have had mothers who bless children even if they are not their biological children.

What about my Lord for I know my Lord loves me and maybe would give me another chance in life if I could solve the murder mystery of the two beloveds from 1866. Or maybe I have another mystery I must resolve. Where was I? Why could no one hear or see me?

As I have walked the streets of New Orleans for over a hundred years, tonight I the ghost bride am still dressed in my wedding gown. I have strolled through the busy streets again, but I don't know exactly how long I have been walking or strolling the nocturnal city as I have lost count of my time. All I know is ever since I drowned in the cold Mississippi River, I have found myself walking through the busy streets of this busy city. It is strange no one can see me nor hear my words. I have screamed and tried to sing songs. I have also tried to talk to dogs and pets yet no one, not even the animals could see me.

The same man who had killed us now walked around the famous Bourbon Street. He seemed much younger, yet I knew the time was not in my period. It was strange as how was he able to be reborn if I his victim have still been living the life of a ghost?

I didn't wipe my tears as I followed the younger monster. I only watched the skies above and told my Creator I would not question him, nor would I cry for I love my Creator even though it seems he did not love me nor was he fair. For how could a monster be reborn and have his ways around terrorizing people if good people don't get a second chance? Again, I told myself not to question the Lord.

The same monster with the same evil traits walked so bravely. His zippers were still silver as he had been busy with another one of his mistresses. He and his mistress walked into a dirty motel room. He was screaming in delight as he was overjoyed with his very young mistress. Naïve and greedy for money, the mistress had a one-night stand. Their screams of pleasure and joy only made me even more nauseous. I ran toward the bushes and threw up. I don't know how I felt sick and all the pains of a human, yet I was only a ghost.

I questioned why a young woman would willingly give away her love and joy to a one-night stand where all the virtues were sold. I tried not to watch them as I walked away. Somehow, I knew again time had passed as I was standing near the dirty motel room and heard a baby being born. I realized it was nine months after the one-night stand.

This one-night stand gave birth to my beloved Silas. He was not black like last time but a white baby boy. I remembered he had told me to recognize him in any form. I did recognize you, but my beloved, how will you recognize me as I am still your bride walking around as a ghost?

How did I recognize him, you all wonder? How could I not as this was my twin flame. He was born, yet where was I? And why had I not been reborn?

Yes, born in New Orleans tonight after waiting so long was the illegitimate child of the famous businessman Drake Crow. The same businessman had in another lifetime murdered the man he just sired as his illegitimate child. I wondered how life was fair. Yet again, I will not question my Lord, nor will I cry and ask for justice.

The mighty businessman who was now in his twenties dumped the naïve mistress who had given birth to the newborn in the dirty motel room. She waited days to prove his identity and that the baby was the son of the rich businessman. A poor prostitute, however, could do nothing to prove the identity of her child's father. It's strange being a ghost as I can only follow some things and I guess my timeline too adjusts to what I am to see or be a witness to, or places I could be.

The young businessman whose name is still Drake Crow like in his last life, bought off all around him and refused to pay for the child. The prostitute without any thought or care, dumped the newborn child in the dumpster. She never wanted to see him or remember her one night's horror story. She said she would start a new life and told her friends she was going to the "Big Apple" now to try out her luck. She was off to New York City.

She had newspaper clippings and pictures of her rich businessman as she grinned and shouted, "Oh my dear! You won't get rid of me that easily! I will make sure you fear me and live in a life of fear. I will always be a step ahead of you. I will always blackmail you that I have hidden the baby somewhere and you will pay me, but you will never find him as the poor child will be dead soon."

After the prostitute walked away, somehow, I picked up the baby. I knew he was the reincarnated form of my twin flame. I left him at the doorstep of a church with a card where I penned his name from 1866. I wrote the child is the illegitimate son of Drake Crow and his name is Silas Coleridge Vivour. I left the card with invisible teardrops that fell yet were unseen and unfelt on the card.

I kissed the card and gave it all my blessings as I watched the nuns take the baby in a basket inside. I trembled in fear and didn't enter the church as I didn't want the curses that I live with to touch the innocent baby boy. What if the nuns question me if I committed suicide or not? How could I explain to them my ill fate?

I heard one of the nuns say, "At least this baby is alive and not left on the road to be dead like the baby girl we found. I feel terrible the baby had to die. Or maybe died. I hope James was able to do something. At least he will pray and care for the ill-fated child."

A ghost bride, who died on my wedding night, I was killed in New Orleans by the same businessman who today left my twin flame on the road because my beloved was his illegitimate child. He will remember my name as he had murdered both of us in another lifetime and today, I watched him in the twentieth century dump his own son. I will haunt him in his dreams and remind him of his evil actions from his past life and this life.

I cried with my dry ghostly tears failing to fall and thought, once upon a time, we were both happily married during the New Orleans Massacre in 1866. Today in the twentieth century, I witnessed a birth of only half of the twin flames. My twin flame was born on a big and crowded night. This was the night of the big carnival, Mardi Gras.

I knew I would not be born with him in this lifetime, as I was left in the dark corner of this world to help him on his journey through life. I knew we would unite if not in this life, then in another. I would never be unhappy or give up as I knew my Lord accepted my prayers. If I couldn't be with him, then I could be a guide for him through his journey of life.

No tears would be spilled as I would be the loving bride who would be his even if he was not mine in this life. I knew I must guide him as he had no one to guide him through the journey of this lonely life.

Come and join me as I tell you about my tale from beyond the grave through this magical diary of mine as I guide my beloved through the darkness to the light. In this life, he is fighting another humanitarian crisis called ageism as he tries to deal with his lost memories of the murders of two beloveds all in the same diary, written by his ghost bride.

I am Viviana Stella (Froster) Vivour and this is my diary. I call this diary "The Bride" as this is my diary, and I am the ghost bride of New Orleans.

THE GHOST BRIDE OF NEW ORLEANS

I lived only for you, my beloved.

I died with you, my beloved.

I searched for you

Under the Mississippi River.

I searched for you above the grounds.

I kept my vows given to you,

As I keep your promises

Given at your last breath,

Within my

Non-beating heart.

How could my heart even beat,

As it was given to you eternally?

I had told you,

My heartbeats are only

For you.

My beloved,

I kept my promises

From life to life,

As I gave you

My oath

To be only yours,

To love only you,

To wait for you,

THE BRIDE, THE GROOM, AND THE GHOST

Eternally.

Now I promise,

I shall be yours

Even if you forget me,

Don't see me,

Or don't hear me,

As I have been lost in

Time.

I am under the ground

And you live above the ground.

I am amongst

The dead,

And my beloved,

You are reborn amongst

The living.

I only hope

You, my beloved, keep your

Given oath,

And be mine,

In life or

In death,

As I am

The ghost bride.

For you my beloved,

Eternally,

I shall be

Yours truly,

THE GHOST BRIDE OF NEW ORLEANS.

CHAPTER ONE:

Seeking Protection Beneath Your Wings

"For over a century, I have waited for you dressed as your bride. I walked silently behind you, even when you couldn't see me, yet tonight, my beloved I am seeking protection beneath your wings."

efeated in life, I watched a lonely man enter his dream home, a small three-story Victorian house with a wraparound porch overlooking the Mississippi River in Algiers Point, New Orleans. A ferry boat away from the French Quarter in New Orleans, the house was furnished by a design firm which made sure everything in the home was over a hundred years old. They called it elegent and sophisticated. I thought it was strange how people have moved on to the twenty-first century, yet they still want to hold on to the objects from the past. They call these objects antiques. I call them time-traveling devices we the spirits can hold on to and travel through.

I sat on the lounge chair on the porch that was a wedding gift from my husband. Silas had decorated this same house with his own hands. He did the woodwork and all the staircases and the porch with his own hands. I only wondered if he even remembered our sleepless nights of working together on our home which we never enjoyed as a married couple. Life never gave us a chance. We thought our hard work had paid off as we secretly purchased this home with our hard-earned savings. Each night, we had worked on the house, our cottage by the river.

My family members had brutally dismissed our dream as they rejected our marriage and took away our home by force and lies. It was simple as they never allowed a free black man to buy a house without any hurdles. I heard the man who had murdered us both had bought the property. In this life, the monster who had ruined our life in another lifetime through his family lineage again got this home for free.

Now as he had no family lineage of his own, his house had gone to auction. Life is a circle, and karma works strangely as Silas is the only living son, his illegitimate son. Without any knowledge of his birthfather, my beloved bought his dream home at auction as his biological father had passed away and the house was auctioned.

It was strange as I watched my husband walk out from the auction room depressed, but then miraculously he was called back. Someone had bought the home and had wanted to sell it to him for a minimal price. Silas rejected the gesture, yet the auction house had said the home was his. The person who had bought and resold the home remained unknown. Silas took the miracle as just that, a miracle from the beyond.

I watched him walk into his new home as he was smiling and talking with someone on the phone.

Silas said, "This feels so strange. I feel excited and so lost at the same time. I got laid off because I am too old for the position now. When I was young and tried to get this position, I was too inexperienced. Now in front of me with all my experiences and years of service, I watched them give the position to a total stranger who had no experience at all. I was told they want younger people as now that's their goal. The person who got the job however deserves it as I trained him myself. I am glad he got it rather than anyone else."

My beloved talks with his hands and body language too. He placed his fingers through his silky hair and stamped his feet. He calmed himself with strong willpower and he sat down.

I could not hear the other person or what he or she had said. I only heard Silas say, "Hmm."

He nodded his head and hands as he talked on this mobile phone, which I have seen people use these days. I am a ghost, but I have kept up with all the modern updates. I want to be the perfect wife for my husband when and if he can see me and acknowledges our marriage from his previous life, yet it's my only life. I wonder how he would love a person he never knew in this life. Then I got some hope, just like he fell again for our home from our previous life. Why would he pick this house amongst all the other homes on this world? Who helped him purchase this house as he had no living relatives on this Earth?

I felt a cold gust of sudden unexpected wind brush near me. I realized I was the ghost here yet somehow my hair was sticking up in the cold wind which blew around me. Was it because of the unexpected donor and his kind gesture? I tried to shake off the feelings as how would someone's kind donation be related to a ghost bride who has been walking around for over a century?

I worried if our marriage was even legitimate anymore as he is a different person in his rebirth. Yet my Lord, I am still the same person. How could I tell him I still could not take off my wedding gown? For over a century, I have been wearing my gown waiting for him to accept and remember me. How could I show him my tears which have not stopped for over a century? The memory lane pricks me like thorns of a rose bush. I don't have anyone laying the fragrant petals of roses down the memory lane to walk above.

I only have pain and sorrows as my company. Yet within my memories just yesterday, I was a living person like all of you. Today, I frighten anyone who can see me; however, you're not scared of the real demons that you can't see. It's strange as not always what you see is the truth as I am not a demon, but I am the victim. I'm afraid to go in front of people for what if they see me and scream in fear? I know there are people who can see paranormal activities even though I am yet to find one such person who could see me and not scream in fear.

If only my beloved had known this home too went to auction as people have rumored for years, this house is haunted by a woman dressed as a bride. Yet the hunter who had hunted the people of this house could never ever enter the home. Reborn over and over again, he hunted the same house without ever being able to enter. For some strange reason, he could never enter the home in all his rebirths and lifetimes. It was as if the walls of this home or maybe its residents yesterday, today, or maybe in the future were protecting the blessed home without even knowing themselves.

Then I heard Silas talk again as he said, "I gave up fighting for my rights. I am tired of this battle. I was told if I took an early retirement, they would double my retirement pension. I accepted it and have bought this house which was another miracle. This million-dollar property was on auction for one-hundred-thousand dollars."

Silas stopped talking suddenly and had a sip of cold beer. He placed his beer can down and pressed his pointer fingers and his thumbs. I realized he was trying to control his emotions.

He closed his eyes and then opened them as he continued, "Some unknown investor bought it at the auction and resold it to me for one-hundred-thousand dollars. I paid cash and have my dream home. Remember? It's the same house I showed you. For strange reasons not known to me, I would drive past this house repeatedly. It's as if the house belonged to me or just maybe I belonged to the house. Hey, I didn't have the house inspected nor have I investigated the history of the house. Everything happened very quickly!"

He then placed his phone on the table, and I could hear his friend talking on the other end. His friend laughed and had a very infectious voice. They said nothing for a while as his friend was doing something. I heard a woman laugh over there too. My beloved loved these people he was talking to. He kept smiling and laughed without any hesitancy.

Someone on the other side of the phone said, "Hey! Maybe the house is haunted! Even if it is, don't worry. My family members have become famous ghost hunters around the world. I do think, however, people are afraid of us rather than the ghosts at times. Listen buddy, I told you. It's better to come and work for Big Papa now."

The people my beloved spoke to sounded kind and honest. I only wished they were here close by for him. He needed someone like a miracle to be here with him during his time of need. Again, a cold breeze touched my hair. The breeze felt comfortable. In some weird way, I loved the strange feeling I was getting in my ghostly guts. It was like someone was talking to me. Hmm, I wondered if there was another ghost in this home.

Then I heard the voice on the other side of the phone talk again, "I told you when I was in Tennessee, you are a valuable person and Big Brother really needs your expertise. I am blessed to have worked with you. As an instructor for the blind, you are so needed these days. People don't have experts like you. Big Brother's hospitals around the world need instructors like yourself. Also, maybe you will find the love of your life there, just call it a hunch maybe."

I heard someone say "Antonius, is that Silas? Tell him we will be in New Orleans soon. We were busy for another reason in New York where a child bride needed our help. We have finished our tour through England and Egypt, and soon we should be there. Tell him to enjoy his break until then."

There was a windstorm coming toward New Orleans and I knew some kind of evil force was behind this storm. It wasn't the gush of wind I feel on myself or around me. This was different, like something evil was coming. Suddenly, I felt cold and had a bad feeling about this. I saw the sun was shining yet it was as if there were two forces, one evil and one good, fighting with one another somewhere out there. I prayed if there was evil let there be good too. I felt very low and knew if only I could have fought the evil myself.

Why are ghosts always known as evil? Maybe someone like me dies and is a good person who needs help finding his or her way. Do ghosts get tired? I do, and I always wondered why? I don't even have any ghostly powers for all I can do is float from place to place.

I watched my beloved was oblivious toward all the unnatural storms brewing outside as he smiled and said, "Jacobus, where is your father, my buddy Erasmus? And my gorgeous girlfriend Anadhi? I miss them so much."

I didn't know who these people were, but I did wish they could be here for him before it's too late. I could see his buddy somehow through the phone as I realized these phones were different and people could see one another.

I saw this woman he called girlfriend and her husband on the phone talking with him. I thought she was directly looking at me. She had her eyes on me. As I moved, she moved her eyes. When I tried to move away, she asked

Silas to place the phone in my direction. Anadhi, the mother of Jacobus and Antonius, and I am assuming the wife of Erasmus, knew I was here.

She then said, "Do you know if you maybe have a ghost bride living in your home? Did you inquire about the past inhabitants or if there were any murders linked to this home? I know the questions seem weird but hey we are the paranormal Kasteel Vrederic family members and all the paranormal activities in this world are just another day in our life."

Silas stood up and looked a little worried as he said, "I am assuming you see more than you are sharing but I will wait for you to come here before I panic about any ghosts or even any paranormal activities. Right now, I am being sued by my company for questioning them about ageism. I am a victim of ageism. Yet somehow, I feel like something is going on at my workplace that I am not aware of or haven't been told about. I wonder if they were sued by someone else."

I watched my beloved and thought the guy that took your job too will be walking toward the same path as tomorrow someone will replace him saying he is too old. I will help you my beloved even though you can't see me. Even though you don't know about me, I do know about you.

I know you are my husband and my twin flame even though you don't. My love is enough to want all the best for you in this one life you live without me. Even if that means I must watch you take a bride or be someone else's, I will never stop loving you or only wishing all the life's best for you.

I saw then Anadhi jumped back as she held another man who looked just like Antonius, but a little different who said, "Big Mama! Are you all right? What's wrong? Why are you so scared? You look frightened. Did you just see a ghost or someone you knew or maybe know?"

It was then I watched three men who looked very similar in age jump around the woman whose name I presumed was Anadhi. She looked Indian with long black hair and gorgeous looking olive-colored skin. She looked like their sister's age, not their mother's. I realized there was something different about her and her husband. Her husband was very tall with fair skin, and I believe he had a Dutch accent. He looked like an older brother of the three young men.

Anadhi said, "Oh, I'm not scared but I just know you my dear friend will be in good hands. There is someone watching over you even from beyond or maybe above. Remember at times, help arrives from places you expect them the least. Dear friend, fear not the dead. Rather, fear the living as it's them who are most frightening. Also, the demons are not to be feared as where there are demons, there will appear angels."

I thanked Anadhi with my hand gestures as I knew she could see me and read my mind. I only wondered could she see our history? Does she know who I am? Or how does it work with this family? Anadhi looked like a kind and loving Indian princess who was the mother of three Dutchmen and wife to a Dutch husband.

She watched me through the phone and said, "I see you and I can read your mind. I won't share anything with anyone as then I might cut off the magical bond you have with one another. Also, Silas fight for your right as very soon you will get an invisible helping hand from the beyond."

I knew she was talking with me as my beloved then said, "Anadhi, I am so confused what you are saying but I will be strong. I will fight ageism with all that I have for not just myself but the people who kicked me out. Tomorrow, they too will be kicked out from the same chair they kicked me out of."

The Kasteel Vrederic's magical family hung up the phone as I watched my beloved sit on his rocking chair watching the sun set outside on the Mississippi River. The sky was orange and had a shadow of gray around it. The clouds were dancing in the sky, announcing a bad storm was arriving. I realized I loved the paranormal family members who were my beloved's close friends. I wished they were here to help him as I feared something very dark was roaming around the walls of this house.

The windows were all open. The white drapes were dancing in the wind. I felt like everyone approaching the home would just want to go inside and see the magical interiors of this magnificent home. It was framed with evergreen bushes. The wraparound porch pulled a person to go inside. My beloved slept on his lounge chair on the wraparound porch overlooking the Mississippi River. The backyard of this home had skyline views of downtown New Orleans which sat on the other side of the great river.

There was a huge oak tree with a swing hanging on it in the backyard. A small fragrant rose garden bloomed near the swing. There were bougainvillea shrubs growing on trellises by the back porch. I wondered if these flowers would lose their leaves and be reincarnated again in spring.

Yet my Lord, why did I not reincarnate with my beloved? Why have you forgotten me my Lord? Why has the Earth moved forward leaving me behind? I am lonely and fear being a ghost. I am tired of feeling cold and want to be accepted by you.

Why is it everything changes, the seasons, the years, and even the people, but not me? I can smell the food, yet I never get hungry. I feel for my husband but never can touch him. I see danger looming around him, yet I can't do anything about it. Please my Lord, let me be of some help to my beloved.

I know people love to watch the amazing waves on their sailboats in the river. But I'm tired of being a prisoner of the Mississippi River. I feel suffocated dressed as a bride with my wedding band and wedding vows sealed and protected in my soul, yet never was I loved by a husband as a wife.

My Lord, I thank you for giving me this amazing sight as I see my beloved still waits for me by the Mississippi River as he promised he would during his wedding vows. I heard a roaring sound behind me as I watched a half man and a half monster walk out of the river. He stood in the deep Mississippi River, watching my beloved. I recognized him as the man who had tried to rape me.

He was the reason I had jumped into the river to escape being raped, not commit suicide. He was a monster living in the river. What was he doing in the Mississippi River? I realized he had passed away and now was a monster in the same river where he had committed crimes directly against us. He must think my beloved was the reason for him becoming a monster. So, he must be here for revenge. Oh, my Lord, is he after me even in death?

I had escaped him by jumping into the river of death. Yet he has now risen from the river of death as he followed me. Who will protect me from this monster now? I knew a demon would want to remain a powerful demon. So why was he still after us? Neither one of us could do nothing to erase him from his powerful return.

I ran inside as I broke down in fear. I saw on the shelves was a cross and a Bible left by my beloved. I tried to touch them as I could neither touch a Bible nor could I hold on to a cross. How would I protect myself in this world? I called upon the Kasteel Vrederic family members for help. I called them in my mind.

I heard a voice say, "Dear one, you may call upon my family members who are right now trying to unite me with my beloved. You see we too have been separated for centuries. My name is Marinda, and I will help you for I am the time-traveling psychic of Kasteel Vrederic. My lineage continues through Anadhi and she will come help you when I cannot."

The time traveler warned, "Don't fear the monster but believe in the love of your twin flame. For even though he remembers not, you still do remember him. So, believe in the power of true love and know love is stronger than all evil combined. Someone related to you from the future could be of help."

I went to my beloved as I squeezed myself next to him on his lounge chair. He looked so comfortable with his flannel shirt and pants. He had a soft warm blanket on him that said, "From the girl with the lantern of Kasteel Vrederic."

The blanket had so many children's faces on it, I felt like I was in a magical land. I knew we had wanted kids of our own, but we never were lucky to have any. I wondered how someone from the future could be related to a ghost bride and her very living groom.

His face was angry yet very sad as he cried in his sleep, "Dear God, I have no one on this Earth who I could tell I lost my job because of my age. I was refused interest-free credit. All my credit card applications were rejected because they told me I am too old. I live now with only cash, and I have enough savings to last me until my last breath. Yet I feel like it's not fair. Maybe I will take on the offers of my buddies from Kasteel Vrederic. At least then, I could keep myself busy by helping others, and it would allow me to forget my own loss and pain."

I held on to him as I cried and told him even though he could not hear me, "Beloved husband, I will guide you and try to help you even from beyond. Today though, I'm scared. The criminal who had wronged us in our last life has awakened in this life. He has now moved into my world as he left yours. I am now dead and still in fear of him. My heart beats no more yet it is frozen in fear. I lived only for you, and even in death, I wander around the dark underworld only for you. Please protect me through your love as I am only yours. Please my beloved tonight I your ghost bride, Viviana Stella Vivour, am seeking protection beneath your wings."

SEEKING PROTECTION BENEATH YOUR WINGS

My love, my beloved,

I drowned beneath the river,

Wishing upon the

Stars

Of the

Rivers

Only to

Be with you.

I waited over a century,

For you

To awaken for me.

Yet my beloved,

I realized,

Through

This journey

Beneath the living,

It is I who am,

Asleep,

Under the

Cold river waters,

Far beyond your

Reach and touch.

Tonight, my beloved,

The monster

I ran away from,

To be with you,

Has fallen asleep,

Under the

Same river,

In my world.

He runs after me,

As he

Remembers his evil deeds,

And has not given up,

Even in this cold

Freezing world.

I need you to awaken

With all the

Memories of our love story,

As we are separated by a breath.

Now I need

You my beloved,

The one whose heart still beats,

To awaken

For your beloved

Whose heart has stopped

Beating.

For we are separated by

Life

And death.

Yet with the power of faith

In true love,

My beloved,

I need your help,

As I am tonight,

SEEKING PROTECTION BENEATH YOUR WINGS.

CHAPTER TWO:

The Fire Dragon Rises

"The fear of fighting the monster terrifies me as I called upon the magical phoenix to come and be our guide. For where there are fear and agony, there are the magical teardrops of relief and justice that come after."

T he doorbell rang musically when dawn broke through the night sky. Silas had fallen asleep on his lounge chair on his porch. There was a fire going on in the outside fireplace as the night was chilly yet warm through the gas fireplace. New Orleans in December is mild. During the day, we have around 64 degrees Fahrenheit and at night it is around 48 degrees Fahrenheit. The rain showers did not bother us on the covered porch.

I wondered who had come so early in the morning. I tried to make some coffee and breakfast for my beloved. Neither could I touch the coffee pot nor the fry pans. I wondered why I could not do anything but float when I had seen ghost movies where the ghosts can move things and do stuff around their homes. How was all this fair? I prayed to my Lord for calm and peace, not anger and unrest within my soul.

The gush of wind blew around me again. This time, the wind brought in a mystical pleasant smell. Silas opened the door and we saw a young man in his thirties standing on the front porch. He had on a t-shirt and jeans. I realized that's how young men dress these days. Not at all cultured in my eyes. The young man had ocean blue eyes like my beloved Silas. His hair, however, was very black like the feathers of a raven. He smiled and had all his white teeth out. I laughed as I thought he was a very nervous person who wanted to show all he was very confident. Somehow, I felt like I knew him, but I brushed off the thought as it's impossible for a ghost of my age to know anyone from this time period.

Silas watched him for a while as he said, "Aurelius van Phillip, how do I have your pleasure today? I hope everything is all right at work and you are enjoying your new position. I assumed you have started your job and I sincerely hope you do well. For remember my phrase, we are there for those who can't see yet will through our guidance. I had just spoken to your family members of Kasteel Vrederic. I know the adoption papers Erasmus was trying to get were approved."

Aurelius was smirking, or was he very constipated? Was something wrong with the man? He brushed his long black hair with his hands away from his face. He walked back and forth as I saw he had mud on his sneakers. Something bothered me as he kept staring at me. I wondered did he see me or was he just nervous and therefore was shaking? I could swear if I was still alive, I would have thought he was the ghost, not me.

Silas opened the door wide and asked, "Would you like to come in? I am about to make some coffee and will make some toast or something. Join me if you would like. I know any family member of Kasteel Vrederic is welcome. Also, I hope you remember I was your teacher, so I still love you as my best student."

It was then I saw Aurelius had a bag of something sweet and warm in his hands. I could somehow smell it. I wondered if I could taste it too. I watched Aurelius place the famous beignets and omelets on a plate while Silas made a fresh pot of coffee. The two men now sat on the back porch with beignets, omelets, and coffee as they spoke over breakfast.

Aurelius was the first one to break the silence as he said, "I called Erasmus, and he told me they would be coming soon. The adoption papers mean nothing, just legal documents. Anadhi and Erasmus accepted me as their son, and I accepted them as my parents. I still call them by name and will soon try to get used to calling them Big Papa and Big Mama."

The young man watched me, and I knew if he saw me, then I probably looked younger than him as with ghosts one thing is we don't age. So, I remained young even though my beloved aged throughout the years. I still feel like I too have aged yet when I see myself in the mirror, I see a young woman whom I barely recognize looking back at me.

Aurelius then continued, "I'm sorry for taking over your job. I never intended to take your job. I didn't even know they would offer me the job, especially from the person who had trained me. It was a shock and I waited for a while to accept the job. I don't even know what's going on. I told them I had my own reasons to not accept anything permanent. I spoke with Erasmus and Anadhi and we all decided we would stand against any kind of ageism, so I quit."

Silas was sipping his coffee as he watched the Mississippi River flow so peacefully. He always squeezed his eyebrows when he thought to himself. He also touched his chin with his thumb and index finger. Then, he rubbed his hair. I was shocked how his past-life character traits had passed on to this life. He looked so different as he had fair skin with brown hair and blue eyes. I missed his dark brown skin and black hair. His innocent smiles remained the same. Somehow, he looked so similar though.

Aurelius said, "I was officially fired today after they rejected my resignation. I had accepted the job only two days ago. I had questioned them about your departure. They lied to me saying you wanted an early retirement. I realized later you were made to retire as I was given your job. Strange thing was I had asked for an inquiry into what really happened and if it was ageism policies. As the investigations began, I asked them if they had denied healthcare to you because of your age. It was then I got the pink slip saying I was too inexperienced for the job, and they must immediately terminate my position."

The conversation abruptly stopped as Aurelius walked over and opened the refrigerator to take out a bottle of milk. He then opened a cupboard and found a bottle of chocolate to make himself hot chocolate. He gestured toward Silas if he wanted a cup. Silas just shook his head, gesturing no thank you.

Then Aurelius continued, "They totally ignored the fact I had resigned before they fired me. I never got healthcare myself as I have had some issues from birth for which the insurance companies have denied me coverage. I had a blood disorder for which I was blind at birth. I was under my brother Dr. Jacobus Vrederic van Phillip's treatment for a while now."

The porch somehow felt like a library. Silence ripped through the air. No one spoke and both men in silence ate the beignets. Silas raised his hands as if he was trying to wake up his body which might have been asleep because of the very uncomfortable way he had slept all night. He winked at Aurelius and finished his coffee.

He then said, "I never knew you had a health issue. I didn't know you were blind and now with sight you teach the blind. It's a miracle and either way it should not affect your promotion. I do hope you have health insurance. If not, then I know your brother Jacobus would cover everything in his hospital. I don't understand why you are here though."

I watched both men talk and realized they loved this Van Phillip family of Kasteel Vrederic. Somehow Aurelius was an adopted son of this family. I wondered what was going on. Why did the Kasteel Vrederic family not talk about him? Something was not right.

Then Silas said, "I know I have trained you like I would have trained my own son if I had any. I love and respect you so much and I really don't think you should have quit. Does anyone from the Van Phillip family know about this? I just spoke with them. They were worried about you, but I didn't think they knew."

I worried about this newcomer too as I wondered why his family would not even know about all of this. Maybe he just wanted to do something nice without informing anyone. I would probably do the same. As I watched his hair move in the wind, I smelled the same smell I had been smelling for the past few hours. I tried to look around and see if there was something in the air yet saw nothing. A real ghost I am who can't even see other ghosts around me. I would scream in fear if I had seen any ghosts.

Silas said, "I have taken early retirement rather than being fired. This way, I got my pension and retirement funds. I am fine except retirement insurance doesn't cover everything. That's just discrimination but everyone knows that. I will survive and I hope you too stay healthy and perform to your best. Through you, a lot of people will learn to have vision without their sight. You are blessed to have a kind heart. I hope you help a lot of people, who don't have their sight, see around them. Instructors for the blind are rare and you are a genius the world needs. We don't have many people like you."

Aurelius walked around in one spot as he again rubbed his hair like a nervous person saying, "I have started an investigation against the company on your behalf. I wanted to know if they did this to you because of your age. They told all that you are too old for this job, and they need someone fresh with a new outlook. They were bragging about getting rid of all middle-aged and elderly people and getting fresh hands. When I questioned them, they said I am too inexperienced and sickly for the job. In your case, they questioned your age, and in my case when I questioned them, they are digging into my private health records."

Everything was quiet for a while as Silas and I both watched Aurelius try to calm himself and start to eat another beignet from the plate. He was a real person with a lot of emotions. Good emotions as throughout the conversation I saw how kind and nice his heart was. I placed my hands on his heart as I felt like if only I were alive, then I too would have called him my son.

Aurelius then said, "Our workplace is not allowing younger people to contribute to decision making and are not allowing new opportunities to older people. They also discriminate against immunocompromised people. These interactions with both age groups and people with health problems are discriminatory and should be called out as practicing ageism and age discrimination. I already have another job offer in my family hospital. I have accepted it, but I really think we should not support self-limiting behaviors like these. We should seek advice from a law firm."

Silas like a habit placed his hands in a fold behind his head. He said nothing and was silent for a long time. There was a black bird that flew into our backyard. It sat on the huge oak tree and as if it was monitoring us and listening to our conversations. I saw Aurelius too was watching the bird as he then looked at my eyes directly. I wondered was he able to see me or was he just oblivious toward me as was the world? Suddenly I felt warm as I thought Aurelius was somehow protecting us. I thought then he winked at me, or was there something in his eyes?

Then Silas said, "I agree, discrimination from companies toward their employees because of their age is wrong. Some are being terminated because of experiences and some due to lack of experiences and some because of health issues. At least we were employees, so we had been employed for a while. Talented people are not being hired because of age discrimination and all other discriminatory reasons. I have spoken to my close buddies who are in touch with some people who will investigate these allegations and maybe do something about it. It won't help us, but it will prevent these companies from taking this kind of actions in the future."

The black bird was now joined by more black birds as they were all just watching us. I knew these evil birds were watching me. I felt very uncomfortable as I had a cold feeling again and wondered why these black birds were watching me.

Aurelius said, "My Big Papa Erasmus called me and has asked me to confide in you and let you know I am not your enemy. I didn't take your job and had refused it from the time I realized what was going on. Also, Jacobus my adoptive brother is my personal physician. I have free healthcare at our family hospitals as he is the doctor who had performed my eye transplant surgery."

Silas watched him in shock and closed and opened his fists like he was angry. This was something he had done even in his previous lifetime.

He stood up and said, "So, that's how you know the Kasteel Vrederic family and that's how you were adopted by them. I am so happy you found your family and the best family to have."

Aurelius then stood up behind him and said, "Andries and Antonius were my buddies and now brothers. I was in Tennessee with them long before Antonius got his sight. I was a patient of Dr. Jacobus. It was after Antonius's accident, that I got even closer to them. The whole family was trying to deal with the loss and the return of Andries."

Aurelius became very emotional as he talked about his adoptive family, and he became motionless. I realized the love they had between them was so much more than any words could describe.

Aurelius controlled his emotions and continued, "Anadhi and Erasmus had me live with them when I studied in Amsterdam. I then came back home to Tennessee as did the Kasteel Vrederic's twins Andries and Antonius until they moved back to the Netherlands before Andries's accident. I had spoken to Jacobus a few weeks ago and feel like it's been years since then. Somehow, I feel like I'm having a hard time getting in touch with anyone. It's as if I'm invisible."

I realized somehow the Kasteel Vrederic family members are very close with a lot of people around the globe. They must have made friends wherever they go. It seems like they are a great family to be close friends with. I only wished I could have known them in my lifetime. I watched Aurelius and wondered what was it that he reminded me of someone I knew or heard. His voice sounded so familiar. Maybe because he was blind, he could sense ghosts. Somehow, I felt like maybe in one of our lifetimes, we were somehow related.

Silas started to laugh out loud as he said, "The Kasteel Vrederic family members are good friends to know and be with. Also, if you are invited to their home once you become their family member forever, don't ever let go of them as Anadhi says our hearts beat for one another. I'm sure she will never let go of you as that's why you are now her son."

I saw Aurelius watch the birds crowd and say, "Yes, my heart beats and I am blessed it can beat within others too.

Jacobus said with all my health problems, my heart is perfect. I registered to be an organ donor."

Aurelius looked into the sky and asked, "Is it normal to have so many black birds here? I have a creepy feeling we are in the film *The Birds*. I wondered why Jacobus had called me this morning and asked me to keep an eye out on you and your home. Something is off here. I remember talking with him and then somehow, I arrived here. I guess I am tired from all these work-related investigations. I don't remember how I came or where my car is as I remember driving by the Mississippi River bend. I had seen something in the river, and I heard something. Then, I guess I just came here because everything is blank."

Aurelius glanced at me again as he said, "Look what is that in the river. It seems like a crocodile. Or is it a man? Oh my God! It seems like a monster from the movies. Okay, maybe they are making a movie or something, but I have the creeps. How is it if they are shooting a movie, no one knew about it? Maybe they don't want anyone to know about it."

Silas got up and tried to see what Aurelius was talking about, as he asked, "What are you talking about? Maybe you saw a bird or a crocodile? It's nothing. You're just tired and maybe you need a break. Are you going back to Tennessee or staying in New Orleans? I don't see anything."

Aurelius was watching me as he got himself some more coffee from the pot. He glanced at his phone and said, "I gave up my rental and have checked into a hotel, as I have sent all my furniture back to Tennessee. I was on my way back when I was asked by Jacobus to keep an eye on you for a few days. Or if I must go, they said to stay until they arrive. They are coming soon. I am staying at their hospital hotel. I did buy a house, but I have left the keys of the home for a friend."

Silas laughed aloud as he walked near the tree the birds were all sitting on. He shooed them and they all flew away. A huge black bird came near Silas as it tried to bite him. That's when Aurelius threw his coffee on the evil bird as it flew away. I saw Aurelius moved his hands like the magical wings of a phoenix or maybe I am too much paranormal to differentiate reality from fiction. Yet his coffee seemed magical. If only I could have saved the image for all to see, then all too would say it was plain magical.

Aurelius said, "I will go back to my hotel as I work at the Kasteel Vrederic family foundation hospital now. I am on vacation until my boss Jacobus says so. For the first time in years, I feel perfect and am in the best healthy condition since birth. Actually, from the time I was driving by the riverbend to now, this is the first time since my birth I have had no pain or blackouts."

Silas watched Aurelius and said, "You are also welcome to stay here until Jacobus and Erasmus come here with the whole family. I too have been offered a job in their foundation and have accepted it this morning. I won't pry into your health condition as I know Jacobus is the best doctor on this planet and his wife too is magical. If anyone can heal magically, it's Jacobus."

It was then we all heard a loud sound of crashing waves and a scream that shattered everything even in the daylight hours. The sun was shining bright, and the river was so calm. People were sailing on the river as children could be heard playing in the nearby parks. Yet the shrieking sounds were too loud to be ignored by anyone.

I saw the sailboats were flipping in the river. The children were all crying as they ran toward their parents. No one knew what was going on as all thought the end of time was upon us. Everyone saw a huge monster which had the face of a man and the body of a huge crocodile or a dragon, roar like a monster. The beast was rising from beneath the Mississippi River.

The shrieking evil sounds was of a man who said, "I will find you wherever you hide. Your beloved can't hide you or give you protection as in his knowledge, you don't even exist. So, you will be mine as I will hunt you down until I finish everyone around you for you. You are seen and known by only my eyes as no one else will see or know you. You will never have any miraculous angel near you as I will finish you and then your miraculous angels too will vanish as I will rule from beneath the rivers."

Silas stared at the river, wondering in his mind what was going on. He whispered out loud, "Did I just see a monster, a demon, or a half-man and half-crocodile rise from the river, or what?"

Aurelius stood there shaking in fear as he watched me and said, "We just saw a monster rise from the river. Now we need a miracle, a phoenix maybe to rise and have a paranormal war. We need the magical angel or phoenix to rise now. Only they can defeat a monster like that. I will stay over as I don't want you fighting this demon alone. You have enough on your hands. By the way, a teacher is like a father, so I am like your son. Now where is the guest bedroom?"

Silas laughed out loud, going closer to the river as the monster was missing and all that was left were people running away in fear.

My beloved said, "I don't believe in any afterlife or ghosts or monsters or even in the magical power of the magical phoenix. I don't even believe in any religion as I am an orphan who was lucky enough to take upon any religion or faith I so wanted. I believe we all have one life to live. We choose our path and ways. I choose to be happy and die in peace."

I watched Aurelius walk behind Silas as he stayed close to him and held on to Silas's shirt from the back. I don't know if it was to protect Silas or to protect himself.

He then only said, "Ahem, I believe if my Kasteel Vrederic family members are coming, then there is something very paranormal going on here. You may believe it or not. It does not change the truth. It's just like our previous employer does not believe they had discriminated against us through ageism. Our new employers, the Kasteel Vrederic family members, do believe in paranormal activities all around them. You too will if it is up to that dragon."

The sun was bright and above us as New Orleans had a very sunny day. All around, however, during the daylight hours, people were running all around in fear. Panic had taken over the city as we saw black birds were flying all over the city which was gripped in fear. Only one person had no fear as he didn't believe in anything paranormal.

I wondered how he couldn't even remember his past life as I never forgot mine. Maybe because I didn't get to see the gate of reincarnation and am being punished for suicide even though I didn't commit it. My Lord, how do you judge me so unjustly and give the monster who ruined my life so much power?

That night as I watched Aurelius cook dinner so confidently, I almost forgot all my fears. He made red beans and rice with blackened red snapper on the side. The home smelled like a restaurant. Both men sat to dine at the small kitchen table with a small television set by the kitchen counter turned on. He cooked so quickly as if he was floating and cooking like magic.

On the television, a news reporter was reporting, "Dead bodies have been rising from the river as they are all unnaturally harmed by a river monster. Witnesses are saying they saw a man monster take women. He is attacking them as he harmed them brutally, then dumped them all dead. Investigations are being held if this is a man who is doing this in a disguise or is there really a monster rising from the Mississippi River and committing these crimes?"

I watched the news and as I jumped up, I dropped the basket of fruits near me. The fruits fell to the ground as both men jumped up and asked, "Who did that?"

My diary that I am writing for you all and my beloved fell from my hands as it laid open on the floor in front of Aurelius's feet. My invisible diary was now very visible to the eyes of all living humans. Aurelius picked up the diary with ease. As he held the diary in his hands, I quickly wrote:

My beloved, I am Viviana Stella Vivour, and I will fill in this diary every night as I am not just a ghost but your ghost bride, and this is my diary. I built this home with you secretly in 1866. Please help me and protect me as today you all have seen what I am hiding and running away from. I hope we find a magical phoenix as he is the only one who can save us from the monster. Today, you all saw even in daylight hours in front of all eyes the fire dragon rises.

THE FIRE DRAGON RISES

Life through reincarnation

Is a gift

I never received.

For you, I died as

I promised,

To be yours

Eternally,

In death,

Or in life.

Then my beloved,

How did our

Knots of promises

Get torn?

Under the

Cold river

Of death,

You have found

Another life to live,

While I still live

With your memories

Even in death.

How my love

Did you forget me

In your newfound life,

While I live in death

For only you,

For my oath?

The given vows

I your bride

Had taken,

For eternity,

Will tie us

Together

As I carry the basket

Of forget-me-nots

As my wedding flowers,

Still to this day.

Yet today even in death,

I have found

The monster

Who divided us,

The human animal

Who had taken you

Away from me,

And had tried to

Take away my virtues,

Has come running

After me,

As he has taken an oath

To have me as his,

Without any vows,

Yet through force.

My beloved, please

Save me.

Save my honor.

Save my virtues.

Even though

We are separated

By one breath

That divides us

Through

Life and death,

Help me and save me,

As I am dressed for over a hundred years

As your bride.

I carry as my

Wedding gifts,

Our memories

From the past life.

Today from the past

Has come haunting me,

The human monster

Who had separated us

Through time and space.

Today you and the world

Have all witnessed him.

As all the living and

The dead now narrate,

THE FIRE DRAGON RISES.

CHAPTER THREE:

The Diary Of A Ghost Bride

"The pages of my diary are filled with words, with love letters, with memories of my past, my present, and are blank as I have no future as I am nothing but a ghost bride."

T he morning sun sparkled its rays into our small home too soon, as I watched the two sleepless men read my diary all night. Then they were reading on their computer's historical records of all the women named Viviana Stella Vivour and my maiden name, Froster. They found a lot of stories yet could not find a story about a white woman and black man's love story.

I wondered maybe my love story never made it into the books of history. Or maybe my love story too drowned and was buried within the Mississippi River like we both were. I wondered did the diaries of my neighbors, family, and friends not include my love story? Then I wondered what about the monster Drake Crow? He must have made it within the pages of history.

Even if my love story didn't make it, the evil monster's destructions must have made it. I know the villains of history make it into the pages of history just as the heroes do. Stories like my own, however, get washed away within the first rough waves. I watched the rough waves of the Mississippi River taunt me as the waves kept hitting the bedrocks of our garden.

Aurelius jumped up in excitement as he shouted, "Found it! I have proof of our ghost bride! She did exist in or around 1866 as it says right here. I feel like somehow, I am here to find her. Maybe that's my life's purpose, to awaken the ghost bride. It's like she is the sleeping beauty of our time. I must be her prince charming son."

I went behind the two men who were reading off the computer screen now. There in black and white was written my death report. It read:

December 9th, 1866

Multimillionaire businessman Drake Crow's boat had an accidental drowning. A woman dressed in her wedding dress jumped to her death. It was not known why she committed suicide. It was said her husband, a freed black man, fell overboard accidently. Mr. Drake Crow and his numerous guests had jumped into the cold river water to search for the newly married couple, but no bodies were recovered. The search will, however, continue as daylight breaks.

I saw there was another report which said:

The dead body of Silas Coleridge Vivour, a freed slave, was found. He will be buried near his family members. His newlywed wife Viviana Stella Vivour's body was never found."

I saw tears roll from my eyes as they kept on falling. I felt no water nor salty taste on my cheeks for as a ghost, my teardrops too are just that, ghostly. No one could see me or hear my words. My emotions, my pain, and my sufferings are now nothing. I realized no wonder so many ghost stories are seen or heard. We need some kind of medium, some kind of understanding, some kind of justice.

I want to have my predator prosecuted and charged even in this ghostly world. How could he an evil man live a nice life, and then be powerful after death? How could he have magical powers even in death to go after innocent victims he brutally killed, that he haunts from beneath life too? Why and how is this fair?

Aurelius watched me as if he saw me clearly and said, "I will help you. I don't know why but I feel like I know you. Maybe if not in my last life, maybe in my next life I will somehow be related to you."

I saw the young man who somehow felt like maybe was my own child. I wondered why I felt so close to him. I called him son of a ghost bride if it made any sense.

Aurelius smiled as he asked, "Did I hear you right? Did you just say I am the son of a ghost bride? Hmm, that would be nice. I do believe in miracles and would accept you as my ghost mother anywhere, anytime. Anadhi has to give her permission though because I love her. Anadhi Newhouse van Phillip has my whole heart, and my heart beats only her name. Well, Mrs. Ghost Bride, we do have a bridge that separates us called life and death, but I know that too is a miracle that can be bridged somehow, someway."

I watched Aurelius's teardrops fall on the floor. I floated on top of them as the tears touched my feet. It was so hot and so comforting like the magical blessings of some kind of potion. It was strange that I felt the teardrops. I wondered how I felt the tears of a man who was alive and standing in front of Silas.

Silas watched Aurelius and said, "Ahh, you are too emotional. In your type of work, you will have a lot of emotions to deal with, so you must be strong. A lot of people are waiting for your help. They will need to be guided through your eyes."

Aurelius just listened to Silas but never replied. He just stared at me as he was surprised how he saw me, but it seemed like Silas still could not. Something happened as that's when I saw lightning sparked inside of our small house. The whole room flooded with colorful lights. Then, I heard water gushing inside of the small house as if the Mississippi River had opened her mouth into our home.

I saw seashells and water lilies cover the floor of the house. The water lilies were gathered where Aurelius's teardrops fell. I was standing in front of everyone dressed in my wedding gown with water lilies all over my hair and my gown. I wondered what was happening to me. I saw Aurelius watch me as he had tears in his eyes falling like a waterfall. I wondered why he was crying. How is it Silas said or did nothing as if he saw or heard nothing?

I stood in front of the two men as I asked Silas, "Can you see me? Am I visible or that's just in my mind?"

Silas said nothing. I realized he saw nothing or ignored me totally. Yet Aurelius got up and came close to me.

Aurelius whispered, "I see you and I can hear you. Are you really a ghost?"

Feeling drained and tired, I sat on the sofa next to Silas. How long could a woman travel alone trying to awaken her twin flame? How long could I roam around asking my Lord to forgive me? I then saw a quotation on suicide was hanging on the wall on top of the stone fireplace.

It read, "Suicide never ends a love story for the beloved as it begins the inquiries of the beloved who is still alive."

I touched the wall, and I realized it was the bridge between us. I tried to tell all I didn't commit suicide, but I just wanted to escape from my predator. I wanted to be with my beloved and somehow, I thought I could save both of us. Yes, the thought of suicide did come to my mind and at that time, I did think it was better than letting a monster touch me. If I had still been alive, I wonder if I could have brought justice to our love story. Our love story ended because of a monster who lived in the body of a man. Today, I saw that man hide in the body of a monster.

I wiped my tears and told both, "I did not commit suicide. I jumped after my beloved for my beloved. I will do it all over again for him. I don't fear death but life where monsters hide in human form. Now I fear dead men who hide inside of monsters. How is life or death fair? Dead monsters have powers as they had power and money as nasty humans too."

That's when I saw my diary flew open and had all my words written inside of it. There was a pen that was writing all my thoughts and words on a blank page of the diary. Silas was reading my diary as it was filling up with words in front of him.

Aurelius came and stood in front of me as he said, "I can see you. You are like a glass image of a beautiful bride.

I would say the most beautiful bride I have ever seen. Your golden hair in a bun is sacred. You fair skin is frail, and your dark green eyes remind me of the green grass around the Mississippi River. You look younger than myself, but I keep seeing you as a mother."

Silas watched Aurelius and said, "You are acting weird. Your work called and said you were acting weird, and you had quit in anger. Your landlord Mrs. Abrams also got my number and called worried about you. What's going on? Now, you are talking with ghosts? Why are you staying at the hospital's guest apartments when your own apartment is a few blocks away? Also, didn't you say you bought a house? I bought this house at auction."

I watched both men and worried for Aurelius as he said, "I moved to someplace that Jacobus owns. There, I get free housing with my job."

Why would he not tell his landlord? And what about his family members? Or friends? Does he have none? What about his new home?

Aurelius said looking at me, "My only family members are the Kasteel Vrederic family members. I am an orphan who they took in and like so many orphans around the world they help, I am one. I never felt lonely or lost. As I got the job, I quit immediately. I want to work with people who are facing ageism, the old and the young. I also want to help people with disabilities."

Aurelius walked over to the windows and stared at the Mississippi River for a while. I realized he was very passionate about ageism and disabilities. He made a sound like a sigh, which could mean defeated or like no way would he quit as he would keep on fighting.

He then continued, "I feel like I'm on a mission. My job fired me for questioning them about ageism. They investigated into my personal medical history and found out about my health problems. They don't want a sickly person working for them, so it was easier to just fire me. I don't remember the house part. Jacobus said it happens with my illness, so I forget things."

Silas glanced at his colleague as he walked around the room and tried to see something outside. He waited at the French doors looking at the Mississippi River. I followed his gaze and I saw there was calm in the river. It was flowing gently like it had no worries and had all the time in the world. It was just like me. I had no time limit, and my nights and days just go on.

Silas held Aurelius's shoulders and said, "I really don't care about myself, and I like early retirement; however, I do care about you, and I will fight for you. I will make sure you are completely healed and are happy with wherever you go."

Aurelius laughed and said, "Sometimes we win and at times we fight even beyond the grave. I feel like here we are fighting with something or someone who is calling us from beyond his grave. Watch over there Silas."

We followed his gaze and saw a man standing in our backyard. He had face like a man, yet his body was of a snake. He was staring at something inside our home or at someone in our home. I realized that someone had to be me.

Where do I hide? I thought as a ghost, I was hidden from everyone's sight. How could I hide from another ghost, a ghost who had been my enemy for over a century?

I watched the two men. My husband whom I loved obviously right now was a one-sided love. I wondered why it was I loved him from beyond and carry the burden of remembering him, yet he had no memories of me and of our love story.

Aurelius stood in front of us as he said, "Oh my, that creature looks like the villain of this story. He is so dangerously ferocious. I wonder why he is filled with so much anger."

I knew why he was filled with so much anger. It must be because he had turned into a monster that couldn't escape the Mississippi River. He was a prisoner of the river. His body was half on land, yet his tail and half of his body were still in the river. The saddest part was all the women he had raped couldn't defend themselves from a demon that terrorizes even after his death.

Silas was watching the monster and said, "I wonder why he has half of his body in the river. Is it because he can't live or breathe without being in the water?"

The three of us stared through the French door and were frozen in time. If we moved, the dragon snake would bite us and swallow us like nuggets.

Aurelius stood in front of us as he said, "Oh demon monster, you are ugly. Why is it your ugliness scares me more than your furiousness? If you are filled with poison, then I will become the immortality serum and fight you from beneath the Mississippi River. Come, let's duel! I love to be the hero of this picture and you could be the villain. Oh yes, leave my friends alone."

Silas shrugged Aurelius's shoulders and whacked his head as he said, "Okay hero man, now let's remember we are only humans. He is a monster probably created by someone trying to prank us."

The monster grew larger and taller. We saw his teeth and heard his growls. Something about him standing tall in our backyard got the attention of Silas.

Then we heard sirens and police cars come toward our home. The police, the firefighters, and the ambulances were all flooding our cul-de-sac.

It was then that Silas paid attention as we opened the doors to a big group of policemen. They helped themselves into our home. Everyone walked to the backyard as we all knew the monster was not scared but only shrieked.

It was then I saw Aurelius take my open diary in his hands trying to see if I had left any proof of why the monster was haunting me.

He only whispered, "Who are you after? The ghost bride, her groom, or maybe me? Yet why are you after us as we have nothing to give you?"

I saw my diary was in Silas's hands. As he opened the pages of my diary, it said, "Not the monster but the teardrops of the phoenix are what shall end this war."

I watched my diary was glowing up as it closed the pages. Then I saw Aurelius's hands flew in the air like he flapped and closed the diary. Like a magical door, the monster too disappeared.

Aurelius then said, "Oh well, great retirement for you and me buddy. Now the whole city knows we have a monster in the Mississippi River who sunbathes in our backyard."

Silas walked over and closed the drapes as he told the reporters, "The monster is yours and the story is all yours. We don't want to be involved in any of this as we believe it's all a prank."

He closed all the doors and windows. He pulled all the drapes to give us some privacy. I wasn't worried as no one saw me other than Aurelius and the monster. My diary from over a century ago that was left on the table opened its pages by itself. I thought even though I can't do any miracles or magic, my diary does. It writes out my thoughts and somehow guides all of us. I wondered how. All I saw was on the cover of the diary, there were water drops.

I thought who cried on top of my diary? Like a bolt of lightning, I remembered those were the teardrops of Aurelius. He must have a pure heart as his tears made my diary magical. No one saw these powerful magical teardrops, nor did anyone hear my thoughts. Yet they all saw the page that opened and read,

I was blessed and reborn to guide you through this mystery. I am the diary of a ghost bride.

THE DIARY OF A GHOST BRIDE

Within my chest is written

A historical gothic

Love story,

Where the path started

More than a century ago.

Two lovers concealed

Their love story

Under the skies,

Visible only

To the beloved

Lovers.

Written upon Earth,

The story never found

A home.

The novel continued

Only within the

Blank pages

Of a diary

That never was

Completed.

As the beloveds

Drowned in

The vast and cold

Waters of

The Mississippi River,

The moon's glorious

Lights

Drowned their story.

The pouring rain

Washed away the

Epic love story.

The two lovers were

Separated in death

As they were separated

Even in life.

Yet through my

Chest,

Is written the

Gothic eternal

Love story

The world wanted

To erase through

The death reports

Of the two beloveds.

The world,

The skies,

The mountains, and

The seas

Forgot of

My existence,

Although my chest

Is alive

And shall eternally

Be alive.

In words,

The eternal

Gothic,

Paranormal,

Mystery-filled

Love story

Of two beloveds,

Sealed and reunited,

And brought back to life

Through the tears

Of the magical phoenix,

THE DIARY OF A GHOST BRIDE.

CHAPTER FOUR:

Searching For The Magical Phoenix

"Teardrops are colorless and soundproof, yet they take away the pain as they give life another chance through pain, sorrow, and rejuvenation."

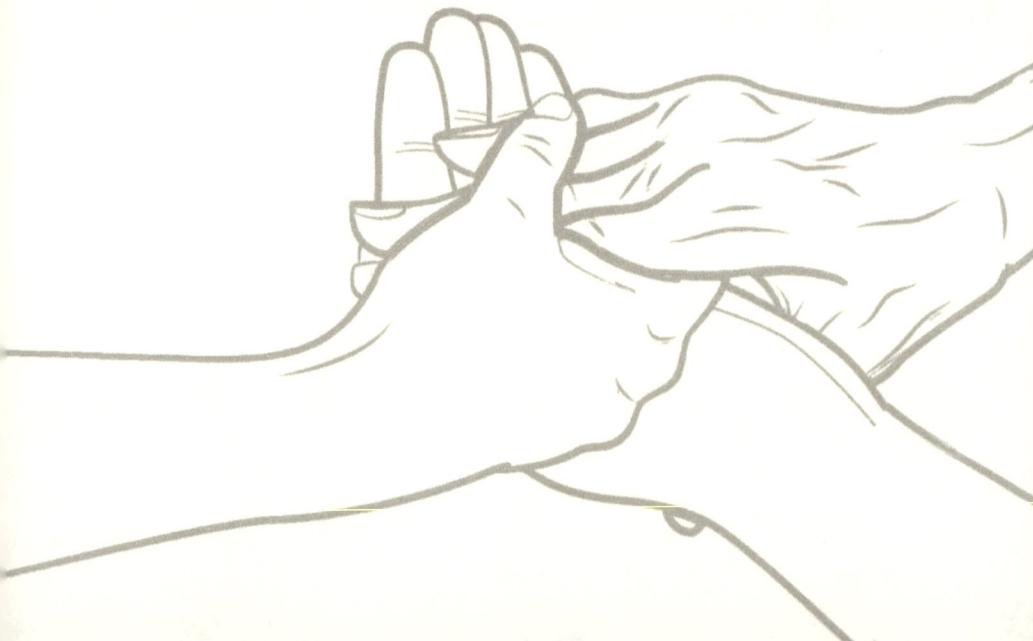

Teardrops of a magical phoenix are something I never heard of, nor did I write that poem. I wondered how my diary was filling up on her own. My thoughts were finding life as they were recorded without any ink or any pen. I wondered how this was even possible. Yet who am I to question anything as I am a ghost bride who has been walking the roads of downtown New Orleans for over a hundred years.

Maybe you have seen a ghost woman dressed like a bride roaming around the famous Bourbon Street. This bride, however, never got to have her groom. This was a lonely and sad bride for this bride never got to be happy. She never celebrated her wedding anniversaries as she became a ghost bride.

I wondered how I had died. What happened to my remains? Did I get eaten by a shark? Or was I buried under the Mississippi River?

Why do I feel like I was betrayed by the humans and my Creator? I was robbed out of life and even in death I am haunted by the monsters. A funny story would be written through history with a ghost bride being haunted by an evil ghost.

Life is fair to the monsters and even death gives them a break. Love seems to be unfair as I loved Silas all my life throughout centuries. I can't forget him even if I try to forget him even for a second. His memories haunt me and keep me searching for a way to him, for a door that I could just open and make him remember me. Why would one twin flame remember, and the other one forget? How could you not remember me, Silas?

That's when I heard a thud and a curse word come from the kitchen. I slept on the couch as I saw Aurelius sleep on the recliner. We both jumped up hearing Silas curse and shout.

Aurelius said, "Oh my, I never thought you would use those words. I thought you weren't aware of those words. It's strange! You are a human after all! Here I was thinking maybe you're like a magical phoenix like the ghost bride's diary's magical poem. Then, you could guide us to the door of solution."

Silas dropped the diary he obviously was reading. I realized I had to think quietly as my thoughts too were being written without my permission. I guess I couldn't give any permission as I'm a ghost and have no opinions at all.

Silas turned all around like he was doing a dance or something as he said, "Viviana, you dare question me? I don't remember you, it's true, but I knew enough to stay away from any woman all my life. I stayed celibate only because somehow, I knew I belonged to someone. I loved that person, that unknown someone all my life, even though I never found her."

I watched him and realized he went in circles as he talked because he couldn't see me. He wanted to make face contact, yet he couldn't as we were separated by death. Aurelius watched both of us as he tried to help us somehow.

Aurelius watched me for a while and then said, "She is beautiful and very graceful. I wish you could see her. It's not fair I can see her, but you can't. I would give up my life to make you two unite, if only I could."

Silas rushed toward Aurelius and hugged him as he kissed Aurelius on his head.

He placed his hands on Aurelius's head and said, "May you live and always be happy. If I could have adopted you, I would have for I see you as my own son. I don't know why. I pray if I ever get the chance to be a father in any of my lives, may you be my son in all of them. Yet I know in this life you were adopted by the best parents a child could ever have."

I saw my tears fell and froze in the air as I too loved that boy and only wished he could be my son through birth or adoption or any way. Yet death is cruel. Death has no mercy for it buries all humans within its cold grounds. Yet it fails to bury the pain away. I only wished I had the magical tears of the phoenix to wipe away all the pain.

Silas somehow watched me. He stared at my direction as he wiped away the tears of Aurelius.

He hugged the young man and said, "She stands right there Aurelius. I can see my ghost bride."

His one sentence made my eternity. He just called me his bride and made all my years of being a ghost worth it, only to be his in life or in death. I watched the love of my life struggle with his words as he tried to see me. Through his words he just connected us again eternally.

Silas said, "Don't spill tears my beloved, I can see you. Your frail cold body is shivering in fear. You are petite and very small, but you are my brave wife. Never ever say I forgot and broke my vows. I did remember and that's why I never married. I've had dreams of a woman running and asking me to help her as she called me each night. She keeps saying, 'My husband, please awaken and remember me. Please help me.' This one phrase kept me alive."

That's when we heard a screeching sound break the skies above. The ground felt like it was shaking as were the skies. Roaring sounds shook our small cottage. I was shaking in fear as I knew the war had just begun. Again, the monster was coming for us. He wouldn't be satisfied that we were separated through the door of death for now he was at the door of death with me as my husband was with the living.

I started to panic and shake as Silas came closer and said, "There is a mirror that separates us. I can see you and hear you, however, there is like a glass barrier in between like they have with patients in the hospitals. We can see them but not touch them."

I saw him and it was so strange I could not touch him either like we had a glass barrier in between us. I could so easily feel and touch Aurelius though.

Aurelius said with tear-filled eyes, "I am so grateful my prayers were answered as you two can see one another. The rest will happen as I believe in miracles."

Silas and I both repeated at the same time, "I believe in miracles."

The crashing waves were making gushing sounds. If we were to get a flood in New Orleans, we would all be asked to evacuate. How would I find my beloved as I am stuck to this area? I have never traveled outside of New Orleans during my time on Earth, so I can't travel anywhere else even after my death.

I walked outside as I stood facing the Mississippi River and I told her, "In your womb I had died. Within your womb is hidden the monster. Please protect us from this beast as he is your prisoner. Guide me and show me what I am to do for am I not buried within your chest?"

I watched the waves come splashing upon the Earth as were the sounds of humans who were sitting around to catch another sight of the monster. The crowds grew throughout the day and night. People made tents to see the monster. I only wondered why people loved horror stories and monsters so much that they were all camping around the river.

Silas told Aurelius, "We need to do something because we don't want people to link our home to this monster. Then they will all come after Viviana as they will somehow tie the stories together. We just need to find out why he is after us. Also, why does my heart keep on telling me Viviana is not buried within the Mississippi River?"

We all saw the monster walk out of the river. As he walked toward our home, the crowd ran in all directions. The brave people waiting to catch a sight of the monster quit their will to face him and were falling all over just by running away from him.

I walked up and told them, "Please don't run and fall prey to the beast. He wants to harm all of you through his fear tactics. He can't do anything because he is dead, and you all are still alive."

96

I realized unlike the powerful beast, I was invisible. No one heard me. Aurelius held my shoulders and as his hands touched my shoulders, I had a tingling feeling as if I had some sense. I held his hands, and I knew for the first time in over a century, I was able to hold someone's hands.

I watched the monster shriek and cry in pain as the three of us stood next to one another. Silas held Aurelius as I too held on to him. We watched the monster jump into the river as he took with him a few innocent women. These women were trying to get the monster's pictures. They did not take his pictures but instead they became his victims.

We entered our cottage and realized people never saw us because there were so many cottages all around. The news channels reported on television the following that night as the news media wrote on all newspapers and the internet:

"The strange Mississippi River monster was sighted once again. People are flooding the area from all over the United States and abroad. The monster is dangerous and had taken some women as his prisoners. The dead bodies of these women have been recovered. They were all assaulted and have died from drowning. All citizens are asked to avoid the Mississippi River until authorities have had time to investigate this horrific crime. Authorities are saying this is a crime made to look like a mythological monster is on the loose but is man-made and shall be caught."

I realized it's easier for humans to not believe in the unknown than to give any thought to what the human mind cannot comprehend. That's when the phone started to ring. I watched Silas answer the phone.

He said, "Hi Jacobus, so nice to hear from you. I was wondering when you guys are coming as Aurelius and I have been waiting to find out what our duties will be."

The man on the other side was quiet for a while as he then said, "The lawsuit has been filed on your behalf and on behalf of Aurelius. Aurelius is my brother and close to my mother and father as they say he didn't choose them as parents from Heaven, but they chose him to be their son on Earth. Right now, we are emotional and really don't want to talk about everything. He was very close to my twin brothers too. I am coming to do some things for him, and I must perform a surgery on a patient at the same time. I hope you are all right as my family members are all very upset and will be there soon."

I didn't understand what the famous doctor was talking about but knew he was trusted by Silas and Aurelius, so I wished to see them myself. The conversation was confusing as somehow something was missing.

Silas said, "Are Erasmus and Anadhi coming too? I really need to speak with them. I have Aurelius here with me. He has been at my house for the last few days. We will be at the hospital soon and will see you there. I would love to have the whole family over here at my small cottage if you would accept my invitation. I could have never afforded this house even with all my pension if you hadn't gifted this to me or told me someone had bought and sold it right away at the auction to me."

I heard a sudden shock of waves and some kind of unrest over the phone as then I heard another voice talk.

He said, "Hey Erasmus here. Aurelius, my son, are you over there? If so, remember to just stay put and we will be there soon. Don't go back to the hospital or your house or the hospital hotel until we are there. Please remember to stay with Silas at his home until we are there. We saw the monster and we know he is after the ghost bride in your house Silas. Griet is here and she said to tell you to have faith in one another. The three of you should stick together until our arrival. Don't go far away from the house, or one another."

Aurelius spoke but it was as if the phone line got disconnected and no one heard him. He was upset because he wanted to hear Anadhi's voice.

He said strangely, "I wish I could have seen Anadhi one more time, just to give her a hug. I loved it when she kissed Antonius, Andries, and me together every night. She didn't care if we were all adults. She said a son is a son always. My God, I love that woman. I can't wait to hold the adoption papers in my hands. If something does happen to me, I want to be buried at the *Evermore Beloved* garden where all the Kasteel Vrederic family members are buried.

Then everything was silent for a while as we all wondered what we should do. I watched my Silas as I thought about how he called me his bride. I could live or die repeatedly with this feeling. My diary opened on that thought. It wrote my last thoughts.

Silas screamed and said, "No more death or horror stories. I have both of you here with me. I want to eat and enjoy the time we have together. Life is a one-way road where we only have one chance to live."

My diary had other thoughts as it jumped up and down and wrote by itself on its blank pages the following:

I am the ghost bride, and this is my dairy. Today, I felt like I was touched by the hands of the magical phoenix. I felt his tears on my hands, or maybe the tears were mine.

He tried to speak but was very weak as he said, "I will stay alive and fight for my life for her life. Jacobus, please come quickly as I try to hold on to life which is now failing my last wishes. How is it I knew about this, yet it still hurts? I love my dreams as I am lonely and now, I see my parents are about to be married again."

I realized this person is about to be reincarnated. Maybe he is in my time frame or maybe he is from the future. Yet in this paranormal world where I feel like I am, everything is strange, and everything seems fuzzy. I feel like my beloved husband Silas knows about me now, but there is a glass wall that keeps my memories and my words from coming to my lips and sharing them with all. This diary that I was gifted by a time traveler from a long time ago, however, keeps my memories and me alive.

It's like my lifeline is in this diary. I can write all my feelings from my dreams or awakened state in this diary. Things I remember and things I forget are all here. So, if I am reading this diary with Aurelius and Silas, then who is the phoenix we all seek and why and how is he dying? For with his death and with spilled tears, the phoenix shall rise and shall kill the monster. Yet it will be very painful. Remember through the door of reincarnation, however, is the way he would become the rising phoenix the monster fears.

Without touching my diary or touching a pen, my thoughts were being written in the diary:

I don't want any innocent person to die to unite my beloved with me. I am dead and I know it's not the path to reunite with anyone. Even if one is alive for a day, that day is immortal through memories. Please keep all friends safe and may no one be touched by death until it's their time. Let's try to save the magical phoenix.

Please Silas, if you love me, then find the magical phoenix to save him. I won't remember everything, but please can we try to save him? Remember our only hope, the only way we can save one another, and an innocent life, is by finding and searching for the magical phoenix.

SEARCHING FOR THE MAGICAL
PHOENIX

Rising from the ashes,

Ending all duties

Of life,

Completing one cycle

Of life,

You grow wings.

You become immortal

As with your sacrifice,

You are remembered,

For your sacrifice

We are united,

Yet with you,

For you,

We all are,

You spread your tears

To save us.

We spread tears

To be with you.

Who are you?

Where are you?

This everlasting bond

We have tied,

Without any blood,

Or without any bond,

Has made our,

Love for you immortal

As you have become

Immortal

Through your sacrifice.

We now shall sacrifice everything

As we are aware

Nothing is a sacrifice,

Where there is love,

Where there is honesty,

Where there is truth,

And where there is just.

Now we shall unite for

One another as we seek,

You through our

Love for you,

And your love for us.

Know this today and forever,

We began this journey not to save

Ourselves,

But you,

The immortal,

THE BRIDE, THE GROOM, AND THE GHOST

As we began

SEARCHING FOR THE MAGICAL PHOENIX.

CHAPTER FIVE:

The Vrederic Hospital

"Who are the dead and who are the living, are the perspectives of the perceivers. For are you the questioners living above or beyond the ground, or maybe you live within the land of the dreamers?"

awn arrived too soon. I wondered how it made any difference to me. Day or night, everything seemed the same where I was. Silas slept like he was having a nightmare. He sat up screaming, "Aurelius" a few times. It was strange watching him sleep so restlessly. I wished I could have held him while he slept. The sun's pouring glares bothered him, but it didn't bother me.

I did wonder where Aurelius was as I had seen him walk around the small cottage all night. He looked tired and at times looked he would be sick. I asked him if he was all right, but I wondered if he heard me or not. Maybe he was sleepwalking. I touched his shoulders when he passed me.

He stopped and saw me for a while and said, "I really thought I was a ghost. Strange thing, I was trying to go somewhere but thought I was getting lost. I kept calling Jacobus for help. It was so strange. I wasn't scared for myself but someone else. I knew time was running out and I must help this stranger somehow, some way; however, I couldn't find the person. I felt like I must stay alive, or else this person too would be dead."

He went to the warm country kitchen. There was a small stove with a kettle on it. Fresh baked bread was there on the wooden table that was set up for three people. Hot breakfast which included buttermilk grits served with syrup, avocado toast, banana pudding cup, and a fresh pot of coffee was set on the table. I wondered who made this meal? How come I didn't even know how this was made or when?

I said out loud, "I only wish I could have taken a sip of coffee. Yet ghosts can't eat. A major flaw in the system."

I watched Aurelius smile as he finished making breakfast and said, "In my dream, I was the ghost, and even then, I couldn't stop eating. I guess living or dead, I love food. So, I eat dead or alive. Maybe you were a picky eater and maybe you still are."

I laughed for so long that I felt my tummy hurt. I said to Aurelius, "I really think you are a joy to be around. I wonder where your roots came from. You have fair skin with black hair and blue eyes. I wonder where you got the eyes from. Maybe your mother was Indian, and your father was Dutch with blue eyes."

I don't know when Silas walked into the kitchen, and he too sat down on one of the chairs in the breakfast nook.

Aurelius watched me for a while as he said, "I don't know; however, my adoptive mother is Anadhi and Erasmus is my adoptive father. Anadhi is Indian and Erasmus is Dutch. I must have adopted them in my heart years ago. They officially did adopt me. We don't have the paperwork yet, but we treat one another as family. That's the closest I have ever been to any family. I love my blessed family."

He watched the river flow outside the kitchen window for a while. I followed his gaze as he said, "Do you remember your birth parents? You look somewhat like a mix of Italian and American heritage. Your skin is fair yet somehow, I feel like your bloodline has Italian lineage. Your beautiful golden hair with brown eyes is mysterious like you have been oblivious to everything that has happened around you. I wonder why you look so alive and not like a ghost. Your feet don't touch the ground when you walk. You float like a princess wearing a white gown."

He spoke about me like I was alive in front of him. Silas took breakfast on his plate as he watched me. Silas had fair skin with brown hair and blue eyes just like Aurelius. I wondered how does reincarnation work? People change their bodies from life to life. Then, how do their beloved family members recognize them from birth to birth?

Silas asked, "Can you eat anything or not?"

I smiled at him as I said, "I don't think so. I would love to have some coffee, but I don't think I can. I don't get hungry or thirsty. Maybe where my physical body is, they are giving me food and drink. Maybe the reincarnation zone is like that."

Aurelius was watching me, and he smiled with his innocent smiles as he walked up and gave me a cup of coffee.

He said, "Hold the cup. I poured the coffee with love for you. If I were your son, you would take it right?"

I got up and hugged him. Again, for some reason, I had another warm tingling feeling flow through my whole body. We were connected somehow, and I could not understand why it felt like he was my son.

I told him, "If I must fly away and become the rising phoenix, I will make it my mission in death to become your mother. I would eternally choose Silas as my beloved husband in all my lives. My other mission would be to protect both of you eternally from the monster as I know the teardrops of a phoenix will save us all."

I touched the cup Aurelius was holding on to. My tears fell on his hands as I saw his tears fell on mine. With tears, we made a bond of a mother and son as I took the cup from his hands. I had my first cup of coffee after more than a hundred years.

Silas came near me as he said, "That's the first miracle of this century. My ghost bride drinks. I wonder what else can she do?"

I drank the hot cup of coffee as then I tried the avocado toast too. I cried as I was able to eat food and drink coffee too. Maybe I was touched by the magical tears of a phoenix somehow.

I told the two men, "Now we must figure out who the phoenix is if it is not me. I thought since I am already dead, I must be in the tunnel to become the rising phoenix. Yet it seems like the rising phoenix is not dead but fighting death. We need to save him. I don't ever want someone to die so others can be saved. I would die repeatedly to save our magical phoenix."

Silas was watching the Mississippi River's tide as we knew the water was rising from all the unnatural rainstorms. He sighed and rubbed his chin like he always does. I wished I had more information about reincarnation and the rising phoenix, and the miracles associated with them. Is it always a miracle when the phoenix rises? The magical phoenix rises and returns to life again to unite with his or her twin flame from ashes.

Then Aurelius said, "Not all humans are lucky to have a twin flame, nor do they unite in all their incarnations. So, they bid farewell and rise over and over again only to unite with one another. I learned all of this from Anadhi as Andries had passed away and returned to her through reincarnation. It was because she believed in this truth and manifested it to be so."

112

Silas sat down and looked very worried as he kept checking his phone repeatedly. I knew something bothered him, but he chose not to share with us.

Aurelius asked him, "Come on boss, what is it that bothers you? We really can't be secretive here as we have a monster behind our home. That's so funny as I thought monsters hide under the bed, not behind the house."

Aurelius started to laugh out loud at his own joke, and we could not keep quiet. Somehow his laughing was contagious.

Silas watched me and said, "I don't know who is going to be the rising phoenix, but I am willing to be one. Maybe that's how we will unite. Maybe that is the only path to my beloved who I too will only marry and be with eternally. I will wait for you until my last breath to only be united in death if not in life."

Aurelius walked up and was shaking his head. I watched the young man and even in this short period of time, I got to know him. I could tell he could keep nothing inside of him.

I asked him, "What is it? Just say it."

Aurelius stamped his foot and watched both of us as he was tearing up and said, "I only got both of you for a short time. If this is all a dream, I don't want to wake up. If this is my future, I want to be reborn here with both of you. If we must live and manifest life as per our inner wishes, then may the ghost bride and her groom be my parents if not in this life, then in the next."

Silas got up and stressed himself. He rubbed his chin and walked back and forth for a while. Aurelius was following Silas's movements. The phone broke everyone's silence as Silas answered the phone.

There was silence for a long time as Silas watched both of us and had no expressions. He nodded to himself, and I wondered how the caller would know what Silas thought if he nodded and did not say anything.

When he hung up the phone, he watched us as he said, "I don't like going back to work but I must as the doctors are all confused. They need some answers from a therapist for two of Jacobus's patients. I'm so confused as to why Jacobus would rush and bring his whole family to New Orleans for these two patients. Even Erasmus and Anadhi are coming with the whole family."

I didn't know this family so I couldn't answer or say why they were coming. Yet based on what I heard from these two men, this family either is very rich or very kind and helpful. Aurelius stood up and wiped his tears which I did not know were still pouring from his eyes.

I let him be himself for a while as he controlled himself and said, "I will come with you and will spend some time with Anadhi, Erasmus, and the whole Kasteel Vrederic family. They are my family members. I never realized how much I missed them until now. It's like I want to go and sit next to Anadhi now. She is the only person on this Earth I found peace with."

I don't know why I felt scared and relieved at the same time. I thought somehow our story had much more to it than all of us knew or realized. There was a storm brewing inside the pit of my stomach. I knew something was going on that scared me more than even the Mississippi River monster.

We all jumped up as we heard roaring outside. Even during the daylight hours, we could see nothing. It was dark and looked like the middle of the night. People were running all over the streets like we were in a horror movie. I worried what they were all running away from. It was then I saw he was standing by the great Mississippi River. Mr. Drake Crow, the monster who had killed two people in his last life, was laughing and screeching at the same time.

He screamed and said, "Your savior the phoenix is dead. No one can save him. He too will be my prisoner as I will imprison his soul in this great river, just like I have kept you two apart, through life and death. I won. You both lost again."

Silas walked outside and laughed out loud as he said, "Fool, you can't imprison anyone even if you wanted to. You are a loser in life and in death. You could never keep my beloved away from me, for I don't fear death and in life or in death I will always wait for her. So, the bridge you fool had created could not keep a beloved separated from his beloved as love is our eternal union. It matters not if she is mine in life or death, she is just mine."

I watched the monster as if he heard nothing and was jumping up and down with joy as he was shaking his scaly snakelike body on the ground like he could not control his excitement.

He then said, "Haha Silas, your phoenix will never rise as he is dead, and the dead will not rise as they only have a few days to rise again. So, I will have no one here even in death who will battle me. I will hide your beloved's body within my memory. She will never wake up or be alive or die with you as I separated her from you. I am free and can be evil as no one can stop me. Your miraculous phoenix is dead."

Like a shadow, he evaporated as the sun broke out from beneath the dark skies. The dark and gloomy day became a bright and sunny day. The people who were terrified and running all around downtown New Orleans and by the riverbanks, were all acting normal as if no one remembered the Mississippi River monster.

Aurelius watched us and said, "I don't know why I feel like I must somehow wake up from this nightmare. I feel the urgency that I have missed something or forgot something. I also must call the lawyer who oversees our case, Silas. He last told me not to worry as he has enough evidence our company has discriminated against both of us through ageism. For my case, however, it was also health discrimination."

I watched Aurelius and thought what was going on? It was as if Aurelius was back in time last week when he was trying to sue the company for ruining both of their lives. I wondered why was Aurelius forgetting we have a serious issue in our hands, the Mississippi River monster?

Aurelius looked at the river and said, "Somehow, I feel like I get so scared that I forget everything. I feel like I'm in a loophole of the time machine. No Viviana, I didn't ignore or forget the monster. I only know we must fight the worldly discrimination fight in the worldly courts. Yet someone must fight the unseen and unheard paranormal monster in the paranormal world. What if our only hope, the phoenix, is not dead for too long and rises from ashes before it's too late?"

He walked away from the windows and asked, "Where are you Jacobus? I really need you."

Silas watched Aurelius and said, "Well, you two could come with me today. I am going to the Vrederic Hospital. I must see two of Jacobus's patients. He said his whole family is coming and should be here soon."

I walked into Silas's car. I felt like I was either floating or had no feeling. I felt like Aurelius too was somehow fighting to be normal. Yet somehow, I knew he was either upset, or scared, or in some kind of pain. I only hoped he was not getting sick again. I hoped and prayed someone somewhere could help him.

No one talked during our car ride that felt so long and was not ending. Then I found myself walking alongside Silas and Aurelius through the cold hospital wing. I hated hospitals before and even in this period I hate hospitals. The smell of clean floors and medical wipes, and the smell of freshly washed hands of the doctors and the nurses make me feel like I would throw up. Maybe it's because I am a ghost or maybe it's just that the hospital wings give people a tough time. Maybe it's because I could smell death. For some reason, I smelled fear and death.

I saw people staring at me who I realized were ghosts. They just watched me like how come I could go from place to place while they could not. I kept quiet so Aurelius and Silas would not see them or fear them. I watched children standing at corners just oblivious. There were people crying in fear everywhere like a ghost ship was filled with crying ghosts. Yet I wondered why people feel the pain if they are dead. I thought you don't feel anything when you are dead. How would a living person know what a dead person feels?

Aurelius then said, "I see ghosts all around us. There are children who are crying and want to go home. Elderly people are upset their family members left them to be all alone here. Why am I seeing all these dead people now? I never saw them before when I worked in hospitals all my life. Now somehow this feels so different. I feel weird and somehow, I am scared."

I watched him and felt guilty as I knew it probably was my fault. For I am a ghost, and all these ghosts were probably coming for me. I wanted to comfort them and tell them to walk toward the light. I tried to tell them, but they ignored me. They kept watching Aurelius. They all wanted to ask him something. I assumed it was because he helped blind people find their way around. They wanted to see if he could maybe help them find the light.

I realized Aurelius was fighting for himself and Silas as they try to win against this world's unjust discriminatory actions. I too must do something and fight for the ghosts and help them move toward the light. Maybe I could make one of the ghosts a superhero who would help all others to walk toward the light. If I knew the path to the light, I would go first and ask them to follow.

Aurelius laughed as he heard my thoughts and said, "We could change roles. You could finish my battle and fight against ageism, and I could be the ghost superhero. You are the dead one and I am still amongst the living. Yet maybe it would be nice to be a superhero."

We saw Silas gave both of us his eyes as he moved his eyebrows up and down. That's like saying he wasn't enjoying our conversation. I watched him and wondered what thoughts went through that mind of his. Again, I got the eye movement. This time he laughed and tried to kiss me on my head, but somehow missed me. He just watched me and said nothing.

It was then I saw Silas was talking with some people as he walked into a restricted area. There was a sign which read in all caps: HIGH SECURITY ZONE, NO ONE ALLOWED BEYOND THIS AREA.

This was a very secured and restricted area. I knew although they could restrict humans, they couldn't restrict ghosts. I tried to go beyond the area and found myself not able to go there. That was so strange. As a ghost, I couldn't even go through man-made barriers.

Aurelius tried to walk in, but he too was not able to walk into the area. Silas watched both of us and just laughed and said, "Jacobus designed this area, so the living or the dead can't go inside. They are a paranormal family and have made this area even paranormal proof. Don't ask me how, but it is."

Silas walked inside the very secured area and what he saw we were eager to know as he spent hours inside of the restricted area. While we waited though, a nurse was talking with another nurse who bumped into Aurelius but didn't say anything. Aurelius apologized but then told me they must be blind as here the patients Silas works with are also blind. They outright did not see me. I didn't want to be the judge but maybe they too were patients.

They were talking to one another as one asked, "How long will Dr. Jacobus keep these two alive? One is dead and still hooked up to the lifesaving machine and the other one has been asleep since birth. I hear one will wake up with the heart of the other as that was the dead person's will. Only the Vrederic Hospital could do this. This secret will never go beyond these doors. Somehow, we too forget everything when we walk out of here.

Aurelius held on to my hands as he said, "We are at the Vrederic Hospital, so no fears! Jacobus will be here! This is my family hospital and now I also work here. Somehow, I feel like I was just here a few days ago."

Aurelius had so much faith in this family, it was contagious. I tried to smile and be happy, yet this cold chilling air traveled through my chest, which froze my inside. I felt numb and just wanted Silas to come and tell me everything will be all right.

Silas didn't come out. Time passed by but no one was coming out of the doors Silas had walked through. I saw Aurelius was walking toward a frame. He touched the portrait in the frame that hung on the wall. There was a picture of a family on the wall. Aurelius was in the picture as he stood holding a woman and a man. I realized who they were as below the portrait were the words: Kasteel Vrederic family members.

Aurelius cried and said, "They placed me in their family portrait. Anadhi and Erasmus said I was not like a son but a son. They were going to receive adoption papers. I know they told me they would bring everything with them. The papers would say I am their son, not an orphan."

There on the frame were the words: Property of the Vrederic Hospital. I was shaking like I had a fever and was about to travel through something. I stuttered and tried to communicate with Aurelius but saw he was frozen and was only whispering something I couldn't hear. I tried so hard to hear him, but it was as if there was a river or an ocean between us. I held on to his hands but felt a jolt of electricity was going through me.

Somehow, I thought Aurelius asked, "Anadhi, where are you?"

I felt strange as I sensed something like electricity tingling all over my body. I wondered where had I come? Why was my soul brought here? What lies beyond this door? The dizzying sensation was stronger as I felt like I was pulled toward a tunnel which was made of light. I was frightful as I thought maybe it was time. Maybe I was being directed to enter the tunnel of light. I, the ghost bride, would finally be directed toward the tunnel of light.

Yet why now? Why must my journey end when I had just awakened my beloved? He could now see me. That's satisfying for me. I don't need to be a physical bride if my beloved knows of me. I could wait for him to come to me and then we could both walk together through the tunnel of light. I must help him fight ageism at the end of his journey through life. I must help Aurelius fight for his rights too.

I cried in fear as I told myself, in death or in life, I only wanted to be yours Silas. So, I was happy as a ghost bride, as I was your ghost bride. I must finish the pages of my diary which I call the diary of a ghost bride. My diary had written on top of it, "The Bride: First Diary." Yet I knew I was at the Vrederic Hospital.

THE VREDERIC HOSPITAL

Ghosts roam around here.

Life is celebrated

With the smiles

Of newborn babies.

As life ends,

The newborns

Are all elderly

Who chose to not

Spread tears,

But celebrate

The beginning

And the end

Of all life.

A place where you

Feel better,

Where you are scared

To enter,

Yet here some come,

Who have devoted,

Their entire life

Making sure

You don't feel sick.

You don't get scared.

You hold

On to them

As they

Never give up

On you

For this place is not feared

By all

As everyone comes here

With hope,

And everyone finds

Blessings

Upon arrival.

Yet those who can't find the

Path out

Of here,

And

Are lost,

Or are stranded,

Within

The walls

Of this

Place,

Or have been walking in

The alleys

Of the dark streets,

Or have been imprisoned

Within

The walls

Of their

Own homes,

Will be guided

Through the hands

Of the family members

Of

THE VREDERIC HOSPITAL.

THE GROOM:

Second Diary

"A story remains incomplete when only seen through the eyes of one perspective. So, the second diary seen through the eyes of the other must take birth."

PROLOGUE:

The Truth

"A diary keeps all the thoughts of a person locked and secured within its pages. It also gives comfort to its author, as it becomes a silent witness, and its words become a written testimony for others to witness throughout time."

T he day had started so differently as I had received a phone call from my friend Erasmus and his son Dr. Jacobus of the Kasteel Vrederic family. It was a phone call I never expected as my life had changed with that one phone call. A phone call you dread, a nightmare that takes away the breath from your chest. Yet this one phone call also removed the Earth from beneath my feet.

The diary of a ghost bride had guided me to this stage of my life. Even though I had never believed in ghosts or the paranormal world, my life had become nothing but a whirlwind of paranormal activities. I found the dragon monster of the Mississippi River in my backyard who followed me from my previous lifetime to this one. The citizens along the Mississippi River had all witnessed this monster over the past few days. Across the border of New Orleans, wherever the river had floated, the monster was visible.

The phone was ringing again and as I answered the call, a familiar voice said, "Silas don't place the phone on speaker. You really don't want anyone to hear this call. Please at any cost, take the two visitors in your home to the Vrederic Hospital. Don't ask anything. We didn't know what to make of this situation, but you must be strong and for their sake, don't say anything."

I listened to the deep and powerful voice of Erasmus. I knew he told me not to place the phone on speaker. So, I imagined he didn't want me to say anything out loud either.

I kept silent as I heard Erasmus say, "You can hear me and that's all I want. Don't say anything but just tap the phone once if you hear me. The two visitors of your home are still at your home, right?"

I tapped the phone once as I heard Erasmus say, "I will be in New Orleans with my family where Jacobus will be performing a surgery. This surgery will involve the two people who are living in your home. At any cost, take both to the hospital. We will explain everything when we meet at the Vrederic Hospital. Please be strong and don't think or ponder about all the things we have discussed as I don't want the Mississippi River monster following you to the hospital at any cost. So, do as I said but forget all that I have said, if that makes any sense. The two people who are there are linked through a very secret surgery both must go through right now."

The phone was disconnected and when I hung up, my ghost bride asked me, "What happened? Is everything all right?"

Aurelius was looking at me with so many questions in his eyes. I did not tell them everything but just that I had to be at the Vrederic Hospital urgently.

I continued, "Everything is all right. We just need to go to the Vrederic Hospital right away. There is an emergency. I would really appreciate if both of you could come with me. I just feel so lonely, or like something isn't right. Maybe you two could be my support."

They did not even question me but accompanied me to the hospital. I followed the instructions of Erasmus and just went to the restricted area which had a sign: HIGH SECURITY ZONE, NO ONE ALLOWED BEYOND THIS AREA. I watched both and told them I will be back soon. I didn't look back as I knew I would collapse if I saw the events that would follow.

I never expected even in my worst nightmare to witness what I saw ahead of me. I felt like I was within the tunnel of life where I would meet my Creator. I only wanted both of my visitors with me as I hoped and prayed for miracles.

In this series of diaries, I too must add my diary. Otherwise, the story would remain incomplete. Sometimes stories must be told from all sides or else you only get the perspective of one. Here the story should be through the eyes of three. So, this is my diary. I am Silas Coleridge Vivour.

I call this diary, "The Groom" as this diary is through the eyes of the very living and lonely groom. As in all paranormal stories, there are so many hidden secrets, but here we will all find out the truth.

THE TRUTH

A groom of a ghost bride

I am,

Yet how do I remember

What is not

In my memories?

From there,

How could I gather

All the lost pages

Of the

Unwritten diary?

All the days,

And the nights

That left us by,

Where neither I

Nor you my beloved

Were nearby,

Yet I knew you were

Like the river waters,

Traveling and kissing

The land

And the different generations.

The land witnesses,

And all the passersby

Know of this love story.

When we are

Buried beneath

The land,

The river,

Or the sea,

Why do our memories

Of our beloved

Twin flame

Fade away,

Or get washed away

By the same river,

The same land

We are lying beneath?

What about

Our love stories?

What happened

When our

Stories never

Found an ending?

How do we begin again

From where we left?

Maybe

Through the memories, and

Through the dreams.

The bridge

Of union

Is made

Through memories,

That were our past,

That bound us

To our beloved

And others

Through

The door of

Rebirth,

That neither could we touch

Nor see.

We only know

Through our

Heartbeats

That come back to us

In another birth

That had stopped,

And made some

Into ghost brides.

Yet how did

The immobile

Heartbeats of the ghost bride

Feel,

Long,

And yearn,

For her beloved,

Very living,

Lonely,

But

Not forgotten

By his beloved

Ghost bride

As she waits

Over centuries,

For

I the groom,

Who was unaware

Of

THE TRUTH.

CHAPTER ONE:

Separated By Death

"Difference between the living and the dead is only a heartbeat. When my heart beats next to yours, you love me. Yet as my heart beats no more next to yours, you fear me. For then, I am but a ghost."

The glass rooms stood next to one another. They felt like coffin boxes but were rooms. The rooms were made of glass and had drapes giving them privacy. No one spoke there nor was anyone allowed to come in without a very special gown which I had never seen. I walked through the very cold hallway that was so different from any hospital wings I had ever seen in my entire life. This wing was designed by the immortal Kasteel Vrederic family members who all stop aging at thirty.

This paranormal family, however, was treating people who are very mortal. You would think being treated by an immortal being was going to make everything easy, but no. This wing felt dreary and frightening. There were either dead bodies or near-death people sleeping there. The objective was to take them through their last period of life gracefully, without any fear or any sorrow but with the knowledge that everything will be all right.

Dr. Jacobus, his wife Dr. Margriete van Achthoven van Phillip, and their entire family worked nonstop all around the world to give all humans a better and healthy life. Erasmus, his wife Anadhi, and their family members travel around the world trying to guide people through death and life. I appreciated how today I would meet my family friends again.

I knew this trip was not something any one of us had planned. Anadhi was really upset, and Jacobus had warned me his mother was really in a heartbroken stage. I didn't know why though. She asked me about Aurelius, and I assured her he was doing just fine. She never knew nor met Viviana my ghost bride. So, I was worried why Anadhi was upset. I only hoped I could get some of Erasmus's confidence and calmness. During any situation, he somehow handles everything. Like maybe he has a magic eraser that erases all obstacles away.

I passed so many glass rooms, I lost count. As I ended up at the corner of the hallway, there were two rooms which had a warning sign on them. The sign read: Do Not Enter! I wondered why it felt like I was somehow related to both rooms. I called my ghost bride in my mind and hoped she could come and give me some support. I wondered if I could bring Aurelius in here as he would be working in here soon.

Aurelius was excited to work here. I know he quit his regular job as they discriminated against me. I would talk with his regular workers as soon as all of this was behind me. I wanted them to rehire him as he is the best and certainly

143

not inexperienced nor young. I also knew they could not discriminate against whatever immunocompromised situation he had.

At the end of the corridor, I met a nurse who smiled at me and said, "I am Agatha Newhouse Brown and I work here for Jacobus. My husband James Brown will help you soon as I know Erasmus has landed his plane at the Louis Armstrong New Orleans International Airport in Kenner, Louisiana, a short while ago. They are bringing the family by helicopter and will land at the hospital's helipad very soon."

She had a cup of coffee in her hands that she gave me. We both walked into a private room which felt like a family room. There was a ceiling fan and a huge fireplace in the room. The room had very comfortable sitting arrangements with a lot of comfy recliners and a huge seventy-five-inch television. There was a corner library by the fireplace. I could see there were rooms off this family room which looked like bedrooms. Also, there was a kitchen bar where a gas stove had a pot of soup boiling on it. I smelled biscuits were being baked in the oven.

I said aloud without thinking, "This place feels like home, not like the smell of death outside in the hallway."

Agatha, a very elegant European looking elderly woman with fair skin, looked like she was hiding something. She glanced at her husband James. He was a very handsome, tall, and elderly African man. I wondered why they were both staring at me. It felt like they were both trying to say something but decided not to. I didn't want to pry and ask them anything if they weren't comfortable sharing it. I would wait patiently until they were ready to share.

James said, "I am known as Uncle James. I am Anadhi's uncle by marriage as Agatha is her aunt. We have been managing hospitals like this one for the Kasteel Vrederic family members all over the world. There are so many more of our family members who run these hospitals as voluntary members. We don't see these places as morgues or monotonous but as places that are needed for all of us the mortals. While on Earth, we want everyone to have a safe and healthy life. The phrase is easy. Why fear the known path of life? Fear the unknown path of life, the afterlife, and the return."

I watched both of them and knew they had a lot of life experiences and were a joy or maybe comfort to have around. My fears were less now that I was in the warm company of these two.

Aunt Agatha watched me and said, "Have some fresh biscuits and coffee. It will help with your jitters. The hallway filled with wonderful people are resting and are doing fine. We just need to remember they were either sitting, eating, or even sleeping next to us. Don't fear them as they are now sleeping somewhere else. The bed they left behind is cold, but the memories are warm and shall be warm with your memories of them. Not all of them are departed souls yet as some are fighting for their lives. That's where we come in and try to make sure they get a chance at life."

I understood these two have faced a lot of life and death situations. Who was I to question them or their knowledge? The cold feelings never left even with all the hot black coffee I poured into my system.

The television set in front of us turned on by itself. I jumped up and found a set of warm hands settle on my knees. Uncle James patted me and watched me for a while. He didn't say anything, but I knew he said a lot through his silence.

On the screen appeared two rooms. One room had a person all stuck to monitors and tubes. I could not see the face nor if the person was a male or female. I knew the person was on life support. Then, another box appeared on the television screen next to the first one. That one had

146

another person in it. Again, I could not see the person but just a figure. I saw the person was not attached to any machines but somehow, I could hear a very faint heartbeat. I wondered what was going on. I wondered if I should just ask them what was going on.

I was scared to ask. My mind asked me if I was even ready to hear the answers. I know sometimes the answers are hidden as we won't be able to handle them. For the same reason, the questions are not asked.

I stood up and just blurted out, "Who are they? And why am I here?"

James kissed his wife's head and using hand gestures asked her something. She knew his questions without being asked. She got him a fresh cup of coffee and Louisiana-style fresh biscuits.

He watched me as he sipped his coffee and said, "I love it here. Because the people here all wanted to be here. They know they are loved and not feared as their hearts beat no more. I love knowing we are only fulfilling everyone's wishes. Yet there are some who are here because they are either nearing death or fighting for their lives. For all of them, we fight for their lives. We don't fear their illness or situation as we love every single one of them."

He got up and left the apartment. Aunt Agatha gestured me to just sit and wait it out. I sat down again and thought these were the longest minutes or hours in my life. I wondered if my two guests were missing me.

Aunt Agatha told me, "They might miss you, but they need this separation time. They too must figure out everything on their own as that's also part of the healing and transition. Sometimes even ghosts need privacy. Moreover, some people who roam around after death or in their sleep are traveling through the same tunnel. It's like they say, don't wake up the dead or the sleepwalkers. They need to come back slowly."

I wondered what they need to figure out as one is a ghost and the other one is my friend. How did Aunt Agatha know what I was thinking? I didn't want my ghost bride to leave now for I wanted to walk away through the tunnel, so we could be at the same place dead or alive.

Additionally, Aurelius was young and brave. I wanted him to have a long healthy life through all his health problems. I wanted him to just breathe and have a musical heartbeat. The sounds of a heartbeat of a son or a friend in my eyes are rejuvenating musical notes.

Aunt Agatha made a sigh as she said, "For whatever reason, you think out loud. You voice your thoughts loudly.

I have seen others who do the same thing. Either because you lived alone and want some company even through your words, or you have ghosts in your home who can only hear you if you speak out your thoughts, or you can hear them if they speak out loud. Even though maybe they can read your mind, we are used to these ways of life."

I watched the warm and kind woman as I kept walking around the family room. Aunt Agatha didn't even complain. She sipped her cup of coffee very leisurely. Her beautiful blue dress reminded me of forget-me-nots. She had her hair up in a bun and her teardrop earrings reminded me of a woman who had seen everything in life.

Uncle James came back inside, and he phoned someone. He looked extremely worried.

He said, "Jacobus, are you guys here buddy? The surgeries need to be done soon. I am worried he is getting weak. Maybe a few more days. Not long, before both will have difficulties. They are both here as their souls are here. I'm worried if the souls find the bodies, then what are we to do?"

I didn't hear what Jacobus said. I really wanted to but knew if I was to hear or know about these issues, they would have told me. I had a shiver go through my whole body and wondered who they were talking about. I must somehow call

Aurelius and find out if both of my family members were doing well. Strange, I couldn't see them any other way but as family members.

I watched the long hallway that was just behind the big red door I waked through. I knew within this corridor laid a secret that I knew was somehow connected to me. I only wondered how it affected me and my two guests. I felt my inner fears converted my whole living body into a mummy. I could neither walk nor talk. My feet felt so heavy as if I couldn't even walk if I so wanted to. It was then in front of us, the television set turned on.

We all saw there in front of us was the great Mississippi River. The news reporters were all running as one reporter said, "The Mississippi River monster is out of the water. He is walking by the banks of the river and screaming. He is asking for someone. He is asking where they are. He is threatening to wash away all the land this river touches unless the body is returned to him."

I got up and asked Aunt Agatha, "What body is he talking about? Why is he so attached to a dead body? He is talking about my ghost bride. He could not have her in life, so he wants to have her in death."

Aunt Agatha watched me as she sipped her coffee and only remained quiet. She looked at another monitor as she only nodded. I realized all these windows were maybe monitors and not just windows. They were showing us different roads of New Orleans and Mississippi.

Aunt Agatha smiled and said, "The dead demon could only be fought by a dead angel. Only a dead person could take on a dead person. I am thinking he fears the dead person as that's the only person who could get rid of him. It's strange how an evil person in death too remains evil. I wondered what about the journey through life that teaches us about our wrong in death. In my experiences, the people who die evil remain evil even in death."

She hugged her husband as he sat down and did look worried. I wondered why I found so much comfort in these two when I realized they were humans worried just like I was. Maybe they went through a lot in their lives and now they are just trying to cross one bridge after the other. My heart just knew something was wrong but what was wrong was killing me.

Uncle James said, "The beast fears the dead not the living. He frightens the living but is fearful of a dead person. In his world where the dead roam, he is the king. Yet what happens if a living person who he fears enters his world? He would then have to fight against the one he fears the most.

He fears the rising phoenix as that's what he is trying to make sure never happens."

Uncle James watched me as he got up and went to the window. He was wearing something similar to Aunt Agatha as he had on blue jeans and a shirt which had forget-me-nots on it. The shirt said in all caps, 'NEVER WILL FORGET YOU MY BABY GIRL AHANA ROY.'

I wondered who Ahana was. Even Aunt Agatha had a big A and forget-me-nots all over her dress. Maybe she was fighting for her life.

Aunt Agatha said, "My baby girl Ahana. You can read all about her in her diary *Shattered Wings: Diary Of A Child Bride*. Here, you can take it with you. She isn't gone as she lives on through her diary."

I watched both and walked around in circles. For some reason, I felt suffocated, and I just wanted to feel light. I saw I still had a hospital gown on that looked like a spaceship costume and I wanted to take it off. I thought maybe if I took this off, I would be able to breathe better.

Yet they both said in union, "No, please don't take it off. It's your survival suit. It's like a life jacket for you in here."

Then I wondered why I had to keep the suit on, but they didn't have any protective gears on. Nothing was making sense, or I was just getting paranoid.

Aunt Agatha said, "Please keep the suit on. People in this world keep their differences hidden behind masks, which keeps everything smooth until the masks break off. Keep the gown on as that's what will keep you safe from the unknown diseases that roam here. We are both immune to all these people as we have been treated by the magical hands of Dr. Jacobus, our beloved nephew. Always remember you are only different from everyone in here as you are breathing. They stopped breathing as their hearts beat no more because they are separated by death."

SEPARATED BY DEATH

A breath away from life,

Or is it a breath away from death?

Where is the bridge of union?

Is it life?

Is it memories?

Like the fallen

Leaves

Of fall,

The living

And the dead

Leave behind them,

Connecting

With one

Another,

The messages

Written

In a diary.

Connecting

All with

One another

Like a bridge

Between

Us the living

And the dead,

Are our memories.

A bridge is

Created

From this world

To the other world.

It is a bridge

Of connecting hands.

One hand

Is warm,

And the other is cold,

Yet through their memories,

They are never separated,

Even though

They are

SEPARATED BY DEATH.

CHAPTER TWO:

Never Fear Death

"Walking toward death, we start the journey of life. Learning to live in life, we settle down, yet the message from my journey is learn to love life. Don't live in fear of the end, but live with courage till the end."

T he day became long and restless at times. I wondered how I was breathing when I felt the reason I was breathing for was not breathing. I sat down and had some hot biscuits, then I had a huge lunch, and now I felt like we were about to have dinner. I felt like I was either fed to forget my worries or I was on a plane traveling where the air hostess keeps bringing us food.

I worried what were my two guests thinking. They probably thought I had abandoned them. Aurelius gets hungry and I felt I could not put anything in my mouth thinking about him. I asked him in my mind who are you Aurelius? My heartbeats are saying you are scared. What about Viviana? Was she all right?

I knew Aurelius would take care of my Viviana. Yet my worries for them became so much that I could hear my pulse racing. I wanted to see if they were doing all right or not. That's when I saw on a monitor appeared my two house guests. They were both sitting on a couch. Viviana laid her head on top of Aurelius who comforted her like a son would comfort his mother.

Aunt Agatha saw me as she said, "No, we don't read minds. Like I said, you speak your mind out loudly."

I realized and laughed out loud. I massaged my withered hands with one another as my hands are often in pain from just doing simple things. My hosts said nothing as they sat with one another and were so comfortable just having each other's company.

The phone rang as it broke the silence in the room. I jumped up in a panic. My racing heart started to pump even faster as if it too was in a heart racing competition. That's when I heard Jacobus's calm voice. It was always a blessing to hear his voice, a doctor who never showed any fears and always saw the better side of each story.

He said, "Hey my favorite girlfriend, how are you? Oh, do tell me you and Uncle James are sitting next to one another and are enjoying being together. I miss being there with you."

Aunt Agatha was blushing with joy. I saw she had tears in the corner of her eyes. She didn't even take time to wipe them as she blew a kiss on the phone. I knew she loved our favorite doctor more than words could ever express.

Jacobus said, "I can feel the warm kisses from my girlfriend. I hope you two are emotionally all right. Remember, this is what he wanted. Please before we even think about anything else, always remember his own wishes. I'm having a hard time trying to get Mama calm, but she is strong. Her faith will carry her on. She knew about the ending of this chapter for years now. It's hard for all of us but if we get lost in our emotions, it will be hard for him. He wanted all of us to know he had known about this from birth. Yet he made sure the ending was what we would be ready for. He fought all his life as we fought for him but sometimes even miracles can't change the end destiny. We should be there soon and have everything ready for the transplant surgery."

I heard Jacobus and realized they were talking about someone else as it was regarding a transplant surgery. Not my Viviana or Aurelius. Viviana is a ghost bride and Aurelius is alive, not well but very much alive. There was no transplant surgery involved in my storyline. I was breathing loudly as I took a sigh of relief.

That's when I heard a familiar voice as I knew this was Aurelius's buddy, Jacobus's brother Antonius.

He said, "Hey beautiful, how are you? Andries is here too. You can hear him screaming in the back. Big Mama is sleeping as Big Bro gave her some medication. We should be there soon. Could you have some rice and dal made? Big Mama won't eat anything else when she is grieving. Big Papa is craving your famous biscuits. He is emotional and has had nothing to eat either."

I heard Antonius and Andries's voices which felt so good. Yet I wondered what Anadhi was so upset about. I wanted to ask but didn't as something was freezing inside of my guts. I thought if I ask what my heart fears, it just might become true. So, I won't ask.

Then Jacobus said to me, "Hey Silas, are you there? If so, then do invite your two guests to Aunt Agatha's corner. We call this private suite Aunt Agatha's corner. They will know, especially the bride and the ghost will hear you. Don't talk about your fears to them at any cost."

I heard Jacobus and thought why he said it like that. He said the bride and the ghost. I called myself the groom as my bride is the bride but also the ghost, yet where was I wrong? I wouldn't question Jacobus, there must be more to this story than what I knew. So, I remained quiet.

I only said, "Jacobus, I will invite the ghost bride, but could I also invite Aurelius? He too works for you, as he is your adopted brother. He was in my home trying to solve the mystery of the monster and the lawsuit around ageism. His thoughts were our firm unlawfully forced me to retirement and had hired him. Yet he quit and came to work for you."

Jacobus had made a sound like he took a big breath. I could hear his breath and felt his cold doctor hands from here. I could even sense his eyes staring at the wall like a blank wall. I could never read his mind or even guess what he was thinking.

He only said, "Aurelius is my brother. In my family, we don't have any adopted but just brother. My parents' adopted son is now just their son and my brother. He doesn't need permission to enter our home, our hospitals, or any place that belongs to the Kasteel Vrederic family as all of our properties are now his too. You too are welcome as you are our family friend, yet Aurelius is family. He will come on his own. I am not worried about him coming to our home anytime, anywhere, in any form. In this life, he is ours. In all other lifetimes, he can choose. I'm just worried about his departure and reentry."

I wondered what Jacobus was talking about, yet he abruptly said, "I have a few surgeries I must concentrate on but will see you all soon. Remember things might seem strange and hard as I told you. I will speak of the details only when I'm in front of you, not over the phone. I don't like giving details or describing things to anyone over the phone if I could do it personally."

It was then we saw on the television screen was the monster. Again, he was walking or sliding like a giant dragon by the riverbanks of the Mississippi. Everyone thought he was a Mardi Gras hoax. I wondered what he wanted.

Aunt Agatha said, "He wants to suck up the soul of the only phoenix that will rise and end his evil deeds eternally. His plan is to make sure the person dies but never returns or enters the door of reincarnation and never goes near him. After his departure from Earth, the person will have a few days to take down the demon before his return. All souls who sacrificed their lives for good are pure and become the magical phoenix. They become ashes and they have the ability to return through reincarnation."

Aunt Agatha wandered off somewhere in her own thoughts as she wiped her tears, sat down, and said, "If the magical bird, the rising phoenix, drops his magical teardrops into the river and if the demon is in the river, then all evil and demons will perish and be no more. If the demon now makes sure the person in question never goes through the door of death, he will never be able to harm the demon."

I was confused as I said, "So, he can keep the person alive by magic? That's good, right?"

Uncle James helped himself to a biscuit as he cooked rice and was making Indian dal. He was a great cook and helped his wife cook. They both cooked together. It was strange watching them be here and just ignore how outside the red door were dead people, or people fighting for their lives.

Uncle James watched me and said, "No, it's bad as then the person will forever be his prisoner. He will neither be dead nor alive. As he becomes the rising phoenix, he could then be reborn and have the power to battle the dragon. However, at this stage, he has no power and only becomes the prisoner of this unknown world."

I wished my ghost bride could be here with Aurelius. I missed both. I didn't know why or how I became so close with Aurelius as we didn't have any rebirth or past-life histories together.

Aunt Agatha watched me as she said, "Reincarnation and its miracles are strange. You could be related to someone from the past or the future, and that's how you would be connected. You might think all of this is confusing but just think of the time traveling tunnel which has no time zone but just one time. That's how people travel time through the tunnel of time. I was a nun and had researched a lot into these topics as people had asked so many questions, I had no answer for. I learned much more from my niece Anadhi and all of the Kasteel Vrederic family members, more so after I renounced my vows with the church as I took the vows of marriage."

I thought about the process, and it felt good, so I said, "In my next life, I would like to be Aurelius's son. He is young and I am old so that only makes sense."

It was then I saw Aurelius and my ghost bride both were standing in front of me. I ran and hugged them both. It occurred to me that I never saw them come in. Where did they come from? For a while I wondered if I was so busy in my thoughts or speaking out loud, I somehow missed them. It mattered not as I introduced them both to Aunt Agatha and Uncle James. Aurelius watched the elderly couple and went to them.

He hugged them and started to cry as he said, "When did you two come here? I bought a house and wanted to have my whole family over. But then I don't know what happened. My friend Silas got fired because of his age and I quit because I felt like they discriminated against me because of my age and illness. I don't know what happened to my house or my will. I did send Erasmus everything as you never know with my illness. Time is not my friend."

Aunt Agatha touched his face and I saw tears fall from her eyes as she said, "We got the letter from your lawyers that you left your house to your friend. Jacobus said he will make sure your friend gets the house for the price he can afford. He won't know it's your house unless you show up and tell him. No one will say anything until it's time for him to know."

I watched Viviana take everything in as she watched everyone and said nothing. She went to a corner and just sat there quietly. I wondered why she was so quiet. I wondered who Aurelius left his house to and why he never asked me to help him. I would help him anyway I could after getting out of here. I loved having him over at my home and felt like he just belonged there. Aurelius, Viviana, and I somehow deserved to be together in our small home.

Uncle James saw my eyes and said, "It happens she is tired and does not know what is happening. At times, she will be fine like in your home as the house had belonged to her in her previous life. Yet why she can see Aurelius and he could see her will be clear only after Jacobus comes. Also, if you feel like the three of you should be together, just manifest it and everything will fall in place. Have faith."

There in front of the hospital we saw a thunderstorm come. There was a window through which we could see the Mississippi River. I saw in front of my eyes the beastly dragon appeared. He watched us as if his only goal in life was to harm us.

The dragon shook his tail as I saw the river was flooding the land. I wondered if New Orleans and all the land kissing the great Mississippi River would be flooded. I remembered Hurricane Katrina and thought that was one of Mother Nature's worst furies. She had taken away so many homes and lives. Even after decades, it is still hard for some to return. I never left and never will fear any natural or unnatural disasters. I will be safe and take precautionary measures to keep everyone safe.

I asked Aunt Agatha, "Should we take any precautions or help all the patients find shelters?"

Uncle James smiled at me as he continued his cooking. The smell of fresh cooked rice and Indian Masoor Dal filled the air.

Uncle James said, "Paranormal war is in the mind. Remember he is playing tricks in your mind to let him enter. What is not is just that, it does not exist. What is only is. This demon is playing with everyone's minds. Some things you see are just tricks of your minds. The demon plays with human minds. Yet some of us have stronger willpower and the demon just can't enter."

I watched the storm outside subside slowly as I heard Aunt Agatha say, "Never fear death as it's a part of the journey of life. Never fear life as this journey through life is filled with obstacles. So, there is no fear just complete belief in whatever happens is for the good. Even if it means we the loved ones must go through the time of grief and mourning, remember the departed don't feel anything, but our feelings so let them know you are fine, as that's how they too will be just fine."

I watched the demon and told him mind-to-mind, I don't fear you. I don't fear the worldly unjust people for I am a fighter and will fight for the right against the wrong. I wondered in my mind how would I save Aurelius and myself from this demon? All the while, I must somehow keep a dead ghost safe from death or until I could join her in death. Also, for all of you who are trying to blackmail me by threatening me with death because of my age or unknown circumstances, know this for I never fear death.

NEVER FEAR DEATH

Blessed are those who fear nothing.

The unjust society,

The unhealthy competition, and

The paranormal world,

Are all imposing threats,

To the lonely traveler

Who has no friends,

Who never competes

Against the

Unhealthy minds,

Who fears, yet

Is brave against

The paranormal threats.

Blessed are those

Who can see the

Paranormal world,

Who know where

The demon lies,

Who realizes,

It's not fearful to

See the ghosts.

Rather it's fearful

To know

Someone

Is watching you,

For be the one who sees,

Who hears,

And knocks

On the doors of

Fear and says,

I am the one

Who

Knocks,

Seeks, and

Finds

You before you

Find me.

I don't

Fear anything

As I am the fearless,

As I

NEVER FEAR DEATH.

CHAPTER THREE:

It Takes A Dead To Catch A Dead

"Evil ghosts roam around the world, we fear. Nevertheless, let's be brave as there are good ghosts who too roam around to defeat the evil."

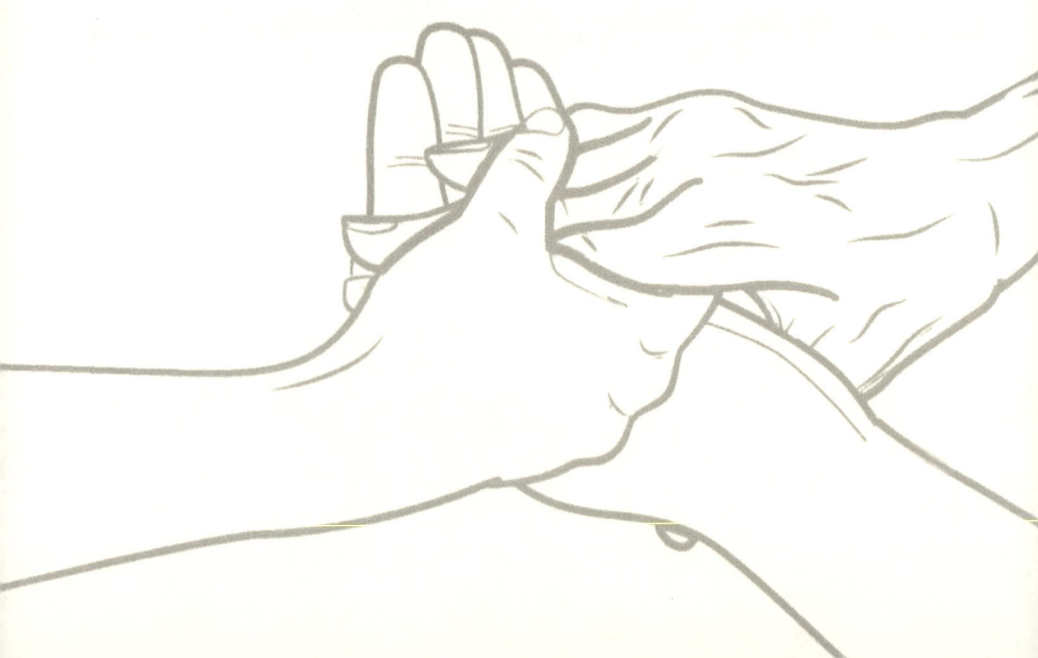

J acobus arrived in the middle of a heavy thunderstorm. Lightning bolts were visible all around the riverbends of the great Mississippi. Three helicopters landed on the hospital's private helipad. My inner stomach was churning in fear. I could deal with the demon, I could deal with ghosts, but I was terrified of letting down the Kasteel Vrederic family members. Also, I feared what secrets they knew I was not aware of.

After being forced to choose between retirement or being fired, I had somehow lost my self-respect. I had buried myself under all different works as I had developed an inferiority complex. Yet I knew Erasmus was my buddy and I was so close with his boys. So, why was I worried? I knew here, I would never be asked to enter retirement in fear of younger people willing to work twenty-four hours a day. With Erasmus and his family, the first rule is justice for all.

I recognized I had become selfish as I didn't know which one of us was dying and who was the living. I was worried about my own self. I knew I must get a grip of the situation. I've worked with blind people. I could get a helping hand from my sixth sense. I would walk with a cane and lean on my sixth sense. I knew something was really messed up. My sixth sense warned me, just to be ready for the worst news.

It was then I saw the red door opened and the Kasteel Vrederic family members walked in. In front of my eyes stood Erasmus and Anadhi. Then, I saw their three sons Jacobus, Antonius, and Andries walk in with their wives. Also walked in six children. I recognized Griet, Rietje, Alexander, and Theunis. The two little babies I did not recognize as they came in their strollers.

Aunt Agatha jumped up and took the little girls as she said, "Ahana Bella and Hana Bella! My little babies! I missed you two so much. I missed all of you too my little ones. Tara Bella's babies, my Ahana's babies."

I watched the older four and the younger two hugged Aunt Agatha and Uncle James. Anadhi was wearing sunglasses in the rain and inside the building which was not like her. She came and sat down as she watched Aurelius and went to him directly. She stood in front of him and touched his face with her hands ever so gently.

I saw she was tearing up as she just stood in front of him. She didn't speak to any one of us yet just stood there pouring her tears out. No words came from her mouth, nor did she move but just stood there with pouring tears. I watched the rain pouring outside as I watched a mother cry for her adopted son. She held him and was just watching him like she wanted to take in all of him, or else she would forget how he looked like in the future.

She said something in Hindi which I thought sounded like, "Tune mujhe chhod ke chala gaya kyun?"

This translates to why did you leave me and go away? I understood Hindi somewhat as I worked with a lot of blind Indian children. She sat down and as I watched her tears pour, her three sons held on to her. I felt like the sky above my head was collapsing as I saw Aurelius just stare at me.

Anadhi then asked, "Jacobus, is my child gone? Or is he still waiting for me? Tell me, please! Is my son dead or does his heart still beat? Please! I can't do this all over again. Andries, I can't do this all over again."

Andries held her with both of his hands and kissed her head. Antonius and Jacobus also held her within their embrace. A few months ago, I had read all the Kasteel Vrederic diaries. I knew how painful the loss of a son was for Anadhi or would be for anyone. Yet everything still felt strange. What was going on?

There was pin-drop silence in the room. Jacobus and his wife Margriete stepped outside of the room. Everyone followed them as did I. We all walked and stopped in front of the two connecting glass rooms that had a sign in all caps: WARNING NO ENTRY.

Erasmus opened a glass door as he let everyone into the huge room that laid behind the small glass door. It was very strange how this room looked like a small home. There were pictures on the dressing table next to the bed. Flowers were left in jars by the huge bay windows that covered the room.

That's when I saw the bed. There on the bed was a young man who was just sleeping very peacefully. I screamed when I saw his face. Everyone watched me and let me just be. I ran to his bedside, and I saw him very clearly. My screams were heard by everyone in the hospital. I recovered quickly as I realized but it couldn't be.

Then I said, "Aurelius, it's your twin brother. Did you even know you had a twin? You're not alone in the world! You have a twin!"

Aurelius watched me as he came close to the body and said, "I don't have a twin. That's my body. I have been dead for a while now. Somehow Jacobus kept me alive for Anadhi to come and see me. I am an orphan who had no family, but Anadhi and Erasmus adopted me like a son. I don't know how this happened. I realized I was dead when I walked into the hospital. I remembered being brought here somehow. I wanted to tell you but thought you would soon find out. The strange thing is I had no clue how I went to your home."

I watched Erasmus and Anadhi come closer to Aurelius as Erasmus said, "These are your adoption papers. It took a while, but we finally have them. We wanted to give them to you personally. Yet you left us without even saying goodbye, my son. I am blessed you can see them before you travel through the tunnel of light. Remember my son, you are Aurelius van Phillip of Kasteel Vrederic, and now you shall travel with this knowledge as we will wait for your quick return. We don't fear death or life as we know it's just a journey. Quick and safe return my son."

The envelope read, "To our son Aurelius van Phillip."

Anadhi kissed the cold body sleeping so peacefully as she said, "Say Big Mama once my dear son, not Anadhi. I waited so long to hear you say it."

Everyone in the room broke down in tears. I watched Aurelius come close to Anadhi and hug her. She saw him clearly as I knew these paranormal family members saw beyond life and death.

She watched him as he said, "I love you, Big Mama. Jacobus, Antonius, and Andries, take care of Big Mama and Big Papa. Also, keep an eye out for my buddy Silas."

Jacobus was standing with his white gown on. I knew how hard it was for him, yet he said, "Time is running out. I must do this now. The operating room is ready and as per Aurelius's wishes, this must be done. Aurelius has left but his spirit hangs around for his last battle. I will do the surgery as you Aurelius must defeat the demon beast before you rise like the phoenix. Also like I tell all, remember to walk toward the door of reincarnation as soon as you walk through the tunnel of light. There is nothing to fear as you know Andries had taken the same journey and returned to us through the same door."

Aurelius had been dead for a while as he was kept alive through a machine that had now stopped, and Jacobus would do his things. Someone was going to get another chance in life through Aurelius's heart. I only wondered who it was.

Aunt Agatha and Uncle James told me in the waiting room who the lucky person was. Uncle James said, "I was in New Orleans some years ago when I saw a newborn baby was thrown out in the road. This child was dumped in front of a church where I was visiting your Aunt Agatha. I am a time traveler and a dream psychic, and I was asked to be there at that time."

He stood up and held Anadhi who she was just sitting there motionless. We worried if she was all right but knew we must let a mother mourn.

Uncle James said, "I picked up the child and took her in even though she was neither awake nor asleep. Everyone told me she was brain dead. Yet as a time traveler and a dream psychic, I realized I had to wait and make sure Jacobus was born. He could treat her. I just had to make sure she would be kept alive until then. I paid for her to be kept alive for years. Like a miracle, she grew older. It was as if she was living but was asleep all the time. Everyone called her sleeping beauty."

I watched everyone sit and wait for Jacobus to do the transplant surgery. We knew it would take hours, but no one moved. The clocks ticked on as we watched Aurelius sit next to Anadhi as a ghost. My ghost bride sat next to him.

Uncle James then continued as he said, "After this incident, the nuns at the church had received another child dropped off there in about a year's time. That's when everyone in New Orleans invented the stories of the ghost sightings. The sightings of a ghost bride. The baby girl I rescued was the newborn ghost bride who like me travels in her dreams. She herself saved her twin flame Silas like a spirit yet fought for her life ever since her birth."

I watched everyone and thought how was this even possible. Anadhi then spoke, "Anything is possible when it's a miracle. My family had kept a child alive throughout years. She matured to be a woman and now an elderly woman. Yes, she is very much alive for this is the miracle of my family members. At times, we can hold on to people yet at times they leave us even though we try with all our might to hold on to them because at the end, it's the Lord's will."

I didn't know what to believe and what not to believe as all of this was too fast for me. We all waited for Jacobus or Margriete to come and say something but all through the night, no one came.

My two guests came near me as they held on to one another. Aurelius got up first as he wiped his eyes and shook himself. Then, I saw my ghost bride was fading as she was traveling in her dreams. It's like when we see dreams and then wake up to find out our dreams did happen during the same time we were dreaming. It's called dream travels.

Aurelius then said, "Now at least we three know who the phoenix is. I am glad I am. But how do I rise if I still have unfinished business left? I will fight the demon as only I can

180

fight him and then rise again. Yet I do wonder why I am able to fight him and how."

Anadhi stood up and said, "Because believe it or not you will be reborn from that same house by the Mississippi River as you had bought the house and made sure Silas gets the house upon your death. You had a car accident in the Mississippi River right after you bought the house. Jacobus and Erasmus kept their words and helped Silas purchase the house from the bank with minimum payment as you left it to him."

I wondered why he would leave me the house. I was the one he replaced at work. I watched him and didn't know if I felt guilty or regretted buying the house. Maybe Aurelius would still be alive if I hadn't bought the house.

Aurelius said, "I left it to you as I felt guilty. They replaced you with me. My own teacher, the person who taught me everything, they made me replace him. I didn't accept the offer and knew my time was cutting near. I was born with an expiration date unlike normal people who have unknown expiration dates. Jacobus had told me I only had a few months left, that too was with a lot of life-saving medication I was tired of taking."

Aurelius stopped talking and I thought I saw tears fall from his eyes. Maybe I was watching my own tears as this young man always somehow made me either cry or laugh. Something inside of my inner soul cried out and told me to just hold on to him. I felt like he should have been my son. The son a father wants but I never had any children or any family. I only wished he were my son. Life around him felt revitalizing. He was loved by all who got to know him.

Aurelius continued, "I tried to stay alive, but I knew it was my time and I was happy to have found you as my teacher. So, as I went to my home, the house you bought. I saw Viviana and I saw you there in the future. So, I knew I had to do something fast. I don't remember how I ended up in the river, but I kept dreaming about you, Viviana, and myself in the house by the great Mississippi River."

Aunt Agatha gave everyone fresh cups of tea and coffee. She made her famous scones for everyone.

It was then she said, "James knew this prophecy. I know Anadhi as a dream psychic did too, yet she hoped beyond hope she would change this part of the predictions. Aurelius, you had seen the beast and went to question him why he was there. He tried to murder you before your time so he could imprison you."

Aunt Agatha stood up and then she sat down again. She watched her husband and I saw he was watching her too. I admired their love and understanding between one another.

It was as if they were one whole together and separated only in life as two humans. The amazing and miraculous bond of twin flames was in front of me. Within all this sorrow, I felt a comfort in knowing Aunt Agatha and Uncle James. Somehow, they brought some kind of understanding and peace to all around them.

Aunt Agatha continued, "A nun from the same church where Silas and Viviana were given to, saw you and called for help. As an orphan, you too were given to her. The same nun saved all three of you. That's how you were miraculously saved by James and me, and eventually entered within the protection of the Vrederic Hospital, not in the hands of the beast. I was the nun you three had come to. Yes, you three, Aurelius, Silas, and Viviana were all miraculously given to me."

Jacobus walked in and watched everyone as he sat next to his mother. He kissed her head and hugged her. I watched her kiss his head back as she snuggled in his embrace. I watched a son hold on to his mother as a mother just lost another son.

He said, "It's all right Mama. He will be back soon, but he must rise like the phoenix for he must do his last job before he rises from the great Mississippi River. It takes a dead to catch a dead."

IT TAKES A DEAD TO CATCH A DEAD

Don't cry, they say,

Yet tears fall.

Don't be weak,

Yet it is hard to be strong.

Close your emotions

Within

A bucket.

Don't open the bucket,

As the teardrops

Too might betray

You

As they become

A waterfall,

Leading to

Your own den.

How do I hide my emotions?

How do I feel for the others?

If I only lock all

My feelings

Within a

Locked chest,

The chest

That beats,

For the chest

That beats

No more.

Why do I feel if

You feel

No more?

Then why did

You but

Promise,

You

Will take

Your leave

To protect the

Ones who still

Have heartbeats

Even though

Your heart beats

No more.

How could I

Take all the pain

Of our separation

When my

Heart breaks

From

This separation?

You have

Taken the oath,

And started

Your journey to

Protect us,

As it's only you

Who can protect

All,

As

IT TAKES A DEAD TO CATCH A DEAD.

CHAPTER FOUR:

Heart Beats Eternally

"Heartbeats never end as they transfer from one body to the other, in another incarnation, making the musical heartbeats immortal."

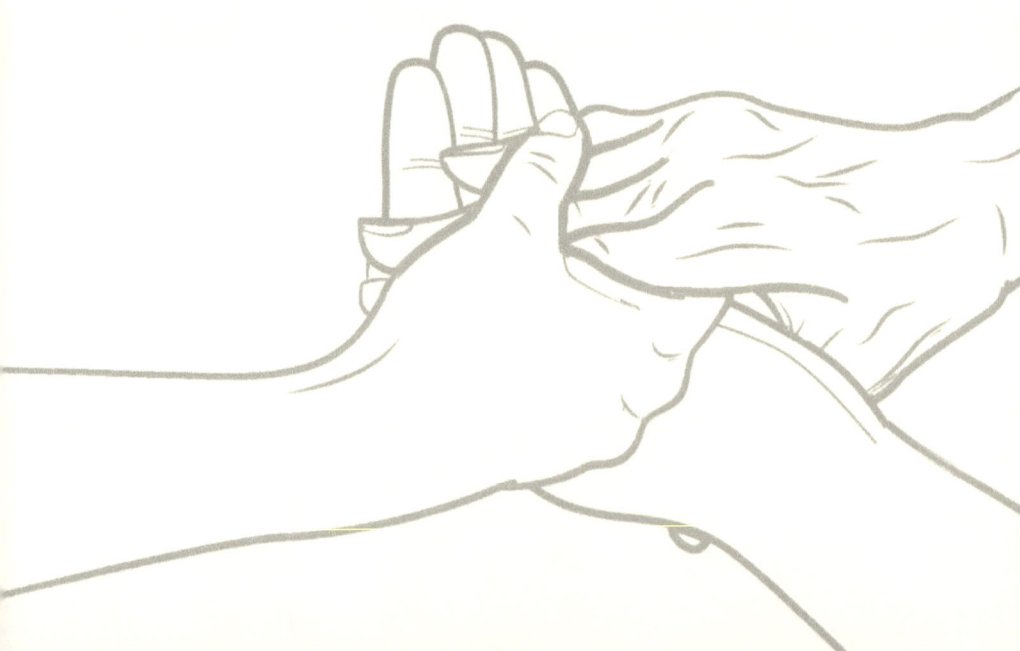

T he hospital felt really lonely as I walked to Agatha's corner all alone. I sat on the couch and wanted to be invisible to the world. I wished I could forget the last few days and pretend all these days were a nightmare. I wanted to wake up from the sleep I knew never broke. I didn't mind the unjust fight I had gone through because of my age. I would take all the pain and sufferings of this one world if I could have Aurelius back.

I felt my eyes betray me as tears poured without any control. My hands were frozen as was my inner self. I realized I was having a panic attack. I wanted to run away somewhere and pretend all of this never happened. I watched a little child walk toward me and sit next to me.

She said in her childish voice, "I am Griet and everyone in my home, Kasteel Vrederic, know me as the girl with the lantern. I guide people back from all troubles of life. Your Aurelius too will come back very soon, but he will only return after he defeats the demon and rises healthy and wise through the door of reincarnation."

I took the little girl with the lantern on my lap as I asked her, "But how do I do this?"

She watched me as did little Rietje, her cousin. They both laughed and said unitedly, "Through your heartbeats silly."

I watched the family members of Erasmus and felt some kind of relief. Margriete came and sat next to me. She placed her hands on my hands.

Then she said, "Jacobus told me to follow my heart for it never lies as we are all humans first. It's all right to feel because it doesn't matter what we do. We are all emotional human beings. Please, don't get lost in your feelings for emotions for then you won't be able to complete the job Aurelius wanted you to finish. Your belief that Viviana will awaken must happen. Your belief Aurelius will be back will only happen through your positive manifestation."

I saw Aurelius and Viviana watching me. I didn't know what had happened, yet my two guests were still with me. I promised myself to work for them now, and not get soaked in my own self-pity. I would mourn and cry after my job was finished.

I asked Erasmus for help as he walked in. I stood next to the very tall six-foot-four-inch Dutchman as I asked him, "Would you help me get justice from my previous employer? Their unjust treatment through ageism has caused all of this. They forced me into retirement because of my age. Aurelius had quit and lost his life because he believed in me and knew age has nothing to do with job performance. If a person can't do his job for any reason, then that's a different issue all together. I want everyone to know how these companies are treating the elderly, the young, and the ones with health conditions."

Erasmus laughed, watched me for a while, and then said, "Aurelius is my son. I already have begun this fight. As my wife said, she and I have lost our son before we could even welcome him home, because this company had treated him unjustly. They said he was too young and too frail. He was the best in his field. His heart was filled with love for his patients. Yet he could not take it that they gave him his teacher's job and fired his teacher. He was a true Van Phillip, and I am proud of my son. He didn't get into the car accident because he was emotional but because his physical body gave up on him. My son fought the world and the beast until his last breath as do all family members of Kasteel Vrederic."

Erasmus walked and went closer to his wife as they hugged and somehow sat next to one another. The love between the two was a love story that will go down history. I loved seeing the bond this family has for one another.

Erasmus then said, "The paranormal demon was the other issue that had caused my son's death, however, if only he was not physically drained, he could have had another chance in life. Jacobus had said he had a few more years to his life. Yet this job drained him out as he was tired of fighting the unjust world. Maybe if he had a better and healthy work environment, we could have had some more time and had some kind of treatment for him. He was sick from birth and after he became an adult, Jacobus treated him biannually. It was his fate and ours. I am proud to be known as his father."

I wanted to ask everyone what was wrong with him. I didn't as I saw Aurelius watching us emotionally. I realized some illnesses were not known as that's why their treatment too was not known to us.

He came close to me and said, "I was born with a disorder. No one knew what it was. After Jacobus took over, I never felt sick. I hated feeling sick and dreaded being at the hospital for days. That's how I met Erasmus and the twins, Antonius and Andries, before Andries's accident. I just want everyone to know I don't feel the pain anymore and I will only leave after I have accomplished what I was born and died for."

That night, Erasmus and his family had left for London, England as they had an unsolved mystery waiting for them over there. They kept the body of Aurelius in a special place so he would be buried in the *Evermore Beloved* garden in Naarden, the Netherlands. As a son of the Kasteel Vrederic family, he belongs with the family until his return, as then he could choose to be born from whichever family he so chooses.

My beloved Viviana was still in the care of Dr. Jacobus and she will be there for a while until she awakens on her own. Jacobus had said these healings take time and can't be rushed. The heart transplant surgery went well, and she was now breathing with Aurelius's heart.

A very small funeral service was held for Aurelius at the hospital which was very emotional. I watched a mother and a father mourn the death of their newly adopted son. Adopted or biological, this family proved it made no difference as love only hurts when separated and grows when together.

I came back home after a very emotional journey to the house which was once bought at auction by Aurelius. Why would he leave all of this to me? I thought I had bought this cheaply, yet I was given a gift from the beyond. I entered the home for the first time feeling lonely. I didn't know how

I could accept the loneliness I was so used to, yet now it felt like it was years ago and dreadful.

I didn't know if I could ever live in the same home that gave me my family and within a blink, like a mist, my family is gone. My ghost bride who was now somewhere recovering from surgeries I don't know of and probably will not know how that miracle even did happen. We didn't know if she would ever wake up.

Also, I didn't know where Aurelius's body was now, yet I only knew his body would be with his family members. Yet why then did my heart cry for him. I had no connection to him, yet why did my heart call for both? I whispered like a prayer I would forever hold on to both of you. For both, my heart beats eternally.

HEART BEATS ETERNALLY

Love awakens the

Jittery

Soul

As the heart beats

Faster.

The pulse races,

Yet then why is it

When the beloved

Soul

Of the departed

Leaves

The body,

The heart beats

No more?

For is it then

His heart beats not

For his family,

Or his friends,

For how

Could love

Die

After the body does?

For then

Does not

The heartbeat

Continue

Even after

The last breath?

For within dreams,

Within memories,

The beloved,

The departed

One's

HEART BEATS ETERNALLY.

CHAPTER FIVE:

The Rising Phoenix

"The golden era or the black balloons are all a belief. Life is only a breath away from death so rejoice life as we all become the rising phoenixes."

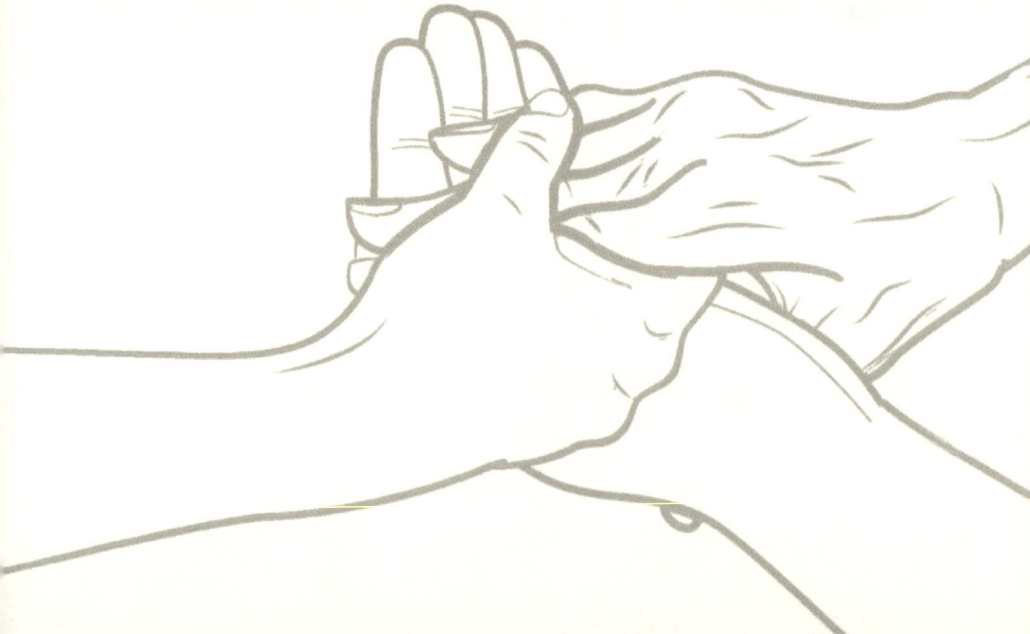

T he doorbell was ringing over and over again. The person at the door was very impatient. Didn't the person not know I couldn't sleep in a lonely home? It's been a few weeks, yet I felt like I just arrived yesterday after losing my temporary family. A small cottage with a wraparound porch deserved a couple and their young son on it. The home too was lonely.

The garden is beautiful with roses and bougainvillea climbing over the porches. Yet nothing felt like a home anymore. I realized the people we live with make a house a home. Not the house. This house is lonely as she too is crying for Viviana and Aurelius. Life must go on, so I walked over trying to let my very heavy legs carry me over to the front door. My legs felt like they too had their own minds and did not want to be up today. Without asking or looking, I opened the door.

I laughed as I could hear Aurelius saying, "Always see who is at the door before opening. 'Stranger danger' was not invented yesterday for nothing. I worry what you will do without me."

The strange feeling of joy encircled me at the very familiar words and then I just ignored it as I knew it was in my head. I wondered if I would really hear him all the time.

It was something I loved but missed so much. There was no sign of Aurelius.

I opened the door and saw the Van Phillip family standing on the front porch. They watched me as if they could read my mind. I knew they could as some of them were psychics. But they never showed any signs of it and let everyone have privacy.

Jacobus walked in with his family members. He said, "Katelijne, my sister-in-law, would like to talk with you as she too was my patient, and a heart transplant survivor. She has brought with her another heart transplant survivor who has been trained and guided by Katelijne for the last few weeks in order to show her how to survive on her own in this hard and strange world."

Behind Jacobus stood his two sisters-in-law, Katelijne and Tara Bella. Both were his patients. Behind them stood Viviana Stella Vivour, my ghost bride. She looked so beautiful dressed all in white. I wondered how this was possible. I wondered how a transparent ghost who had been in this house was standing in front of me in a human form. She looked the same yet had aged like me. I wondered if someone had her picture taken and through a computer did age progression. The young ghost bride had gray hair. She had her hair placed in a bun and walked gracefully.

Anadhi said, "It's called dream travels. A lot of people wake up every morning thinking they have a husband or a wife and a family somewhere else. Or people live through mysteries in their dreams which sometimes they read in the newspapers in coming years. It's happened and will keep happening. People just don't understand this miracle until they too are touched by it. Your ghost bride lived with you through her dreams. So, it's like she was here."

I knew Anadhi and Erasmus could read minds but never shared any details about it. I just laughed out loud as I kissed Anadhi's head. I understood anything is possible in the world of Kasteel Vrederic. So, I just wanted to stay awake and comprehend this was not a dream but reality.

Erasmus laughed and said, "It's not a dream buddy. It's all real. Or maybe we are all just ghosts. You decide."

I laughed out loud as it felt so good to just get the emotions out. I kept on laughing until I pinched myself to stop laughing. Or else, I might faint out of being just happy to see all of my favorite people.

I pinched myself again as I heard Andries say, "Oh, that probably hurts. I know you are overjoyed to see me as everyone becomes when they see me. No need to pinch yourselves."

I saw Jacobus hit Andries's head as Andries said, "Big Bro, that hurts."

Then Antonius hit his head as Andries said again, "Buddy, that hurts! Big Mama, stop them."

Anadhi gave her boys a look and they all knew it was time to stop anything they were doing.

I laughed and felt so good to see them. I hugged Jacobus as he just watched me and winked his eye. He was a very calm and controlled person. I knew this was so natural for him as he was a positive person and he spread this vibe all around the places he went and stayed at.

Jacobus laughed and became relaxed as he said, "Mama and Papa have brought a gift for you. She walks and talks, has also been trained by my two sisters-in-law who had both gone through similar things in their lifetime. She is a miracle patient and as her case is top secret, it is not to be shared or discussed with anyone."

I loved having all of them in my home as it felt like a family reunion. I observed Anadhi was quiet as we had a small wedding ceremony held in the family room with all the curtains drawn.

Anadhi stood in the embrace of her three sons as Jacobus asked, "Mama, what is it? Why all this secrecy? Is something wrong?"

Anadhi looked at Aunt Agatha and asked, "Aunt Agatha, Uncle James, where is he?"

We all knew Uncle James and Aunt Agatha were different as they never shared their secrets with anyone other than this family which was respected. They both watched all of us as our small wedding ceremony performed by Uncle James was over. We had cakes and food brought by the Van Phillip family as everything was small yet very elegantly and very quickly done.

Uncle James watched Anadhi and said, "He is still here. Yet he must begin his war for his name Aurelius means golden radiance of the phoenix like the good one and Drake the monster means dragon-like traits. So now we shall see the war between the good and the bad."

Uncle James watched Anadhi and Erasmus as he went closer to the window and just stood there.

He then continued, "You all knew he was the rising phoenix. The good traits of the rising phoenix are in him. Yet you all should have known the beast, the dragon, too has the traits of the phoenix. The war between the good and the bad is not only on Earth but in Heaven and beyond."

Uncle James stood watching something for a while. I knew they were all talking about my Aurelius. I missed him so much. It felt like a knife cut something inside of myself that I couldn't show nor tell anyone about. I was married to the love of my life miraculously, yet I only wanted to see Aurelius one more time.

Uncle James then continued and said, "Our Aurelius will rise yet before he does rise, he must once more fight a paranormal battle with Drake the dragon. I hear the company he worked and lost his job with has apologized and have promised to pay a hefty amount to Aurelius's family trust for his unjust firing. The company I hear has been bought off by a new owner as the previous owners have filed bankruptcy. A new owner will take over and will reconstruct their whole company with people who believe in equal opportunities for all."

The room became silent as I saw there in the room was standing our Aurelius. He was watching everyone as I saw Viviana go and touch him. She hugged him and touched his heart. Then she placed his hands on her heart. I saw his teardrops fall on her. The teardrops of a ghost fell on my ghost bride's hands. She started to cry as she kissed his hands and his head and his cheeks.

For the first time in years, Viviana uttered her first words as she said, "Aurelius, how is this possible? I remember everything, and I am the ghost bride as Silas is the groom and you are Aurelius the one who kept everything together in our small home. What happened? Why did you leave me before I even woke up? Your heart beats inside of my body."

Our ghost kissed Viviana on her head and cheeks. He hugged her and just stood there watching her like a son would watch his mother. He touched her heart and kissed her head again.

Aurelius laughed and said, "Okay everyone, no more crying or missing me. I'm here and I have a war to fight with the dragon demon. Now we must have some fun and joy in this family. I see my buddies Andries and Antonius are here with Big Bro Jacobus. That means it's family night in this home."

Aurelius watched the Mississippi River as he said, "The river looks so rough, and the monster looks furious. I feel like he knows you both just had the wedding ceremony. Yet in this life, I don't want him raping you like he did in your last life. Viviana, your body was never found as he found it floating in the river and took it home with him. He raped a dead woman and then buried you in his backyard. Find out what Drake's address was last life, and you will find Viviana's body. I want you to give her a proper burial maybe next to my body. Maybe you can have a headstone saying mother and son through the bondage of being ghosts."

Aurelius went to the kitchen and somehow was having bread, brought by Griet the young daughter of Kasteel Vrederic known as the girl with the lantern. She had walked in with a basket of fresh baked bread.

He watched Viviana and sat next to her and said, "When you know what happened is how you move on. It's hard but it's better to get over it. When you died in your last life, you had told him he could never touch your living body. He could not as he touched your dead body. You didn't commit suicide. You saved your honor as a bride. Also, your doctor is still in the house, so get over all your physical and emotional troubles now."

We all saw then in the Mississippi River came up a roaring dragon. He screeched and was causing another tsunami in the river. I wondered what was going to happen now. I watched Viviana get up and wipe her tears as she hugged Aurelius.

She told him, "Thank you. Now, I'm free from the guilt. I did what I did to save my honor and I am proud I had saved my honor, but he proved he was a beast and still is nothing more than a beast."

We saw outside there was a storm brewing again. We all went to the windows, and we ran outside to see what was going on.

206

Anadhi said, "The teardrops of a phoenix will get rid of that monster and all the other monsters of the Mississippi River. For in some stories, it's the love that destroys the beast, yet in some it's the love, the sacrifice, and the tears of separation. Good over evil always wins. When my Aurelius will be ready for his rebirth and gets on his journey is when the demon will become ashes."

It was then we all saw with pouring tears in his eyes, Aurelius was becoming like a fire as we all rushed outside. We saw on top of the great Mississippi River, rose a phoenix. The teardrops of the magical phoenix fell on top of the river. They were not a drop but shower falls. Everyone around the river, near and far, witnessed this miracle."

There on top of the river was flying a magical phoenix. His wings were huge like they covered the river in their embrace. Then we all heard and saw the fire balls came out from the body of the miraculous phoenix. As the bird circled the river, its tears fell on the river like magical rainfalls that just fell and covered the river. The teardrops were made from fire, and we realized the tears were burning on the water over the river. It felt like a gothic paranormal movie we had never seen.

The great Mississippi River was on fire. The river was frozen yet was burning and everything inside of the river became frozen yet burned to ashes.

Aurelius the rising phoenix then said, "From ashes to ashes you shall be. Let the demon be removed eternally as where evil is born there shall always be born good. Let the world witness in all wars that erupt, shall take birth good and evil. Remember in the end good shall always be victorious. As I am Aurelius the rising phoenix, and I shall take birth frequently only to defeat you Drake the demon, the evil."

Then everything became calm as the burning river turned back to blue and flowed calmly. The birds were flying over it as were children and people walking by it. Small sailboats and fishermen were all going on with their lives. Everything went on as if nothing just happened. The gothic movie finished with no memories of it ever being happened. The only proof of the story ever being in existence was in our memories.

Dawn broke through as the Kasteel Vrederic family members had left. My beloved wife Viviana and I celebrated our first wedding night together. For nearly two hundred years, my wife dressed in a wedding gown roamed through the streets of New Orleans. Yet today we took an early morning stroll through the roads of downtown New Orleans.

She was dressed in blue, a gift given to her from Anadhi, which had woven in the dress forget-me-nots, from the *Evermore Beloved* garden, where our Aurelius was buried and so were Viviana's remains from her previous life. With my permission, Erasmus took both back to the Netherlands. As he wanted his son Aurelius van Phillip and his ghost mother to be remembered as their family members.

Viviana and I stood by the riverbank where we last saw Aurelius and knew he was our son, the son we never had, yet today all of you know him as the rising phoenix.

ANN MARIE RUBY

THE RISING PHOENIX

The evil roams around

Not in fear

Yet with anger

And fury.

He never gives up

As he declares

War all around.

Never does he fear

The teardrops

Of his victims,

Nor does he wonder

What happened to

His victims

For all he sees

In the river

Of life are

His own desires, and

His own war.

Yet where

There is evil,

There is good.

Where there is

A demon,

THE BRIDE, THE GROOM, AND THE GHOST

There is an angel

Who is waiting

For you the demon

To see his

Face

In the river

Of your sins.

His

Teardrops

Shall erase

All of your

Demonic wars,

For as his teardrops

Touch your

River of sins,

You and

All your sins

Shall evaporate.

Then,

There shall be

No evidence,

Of you ever being,

As

All shall

Only see,

And remember,

THE RISING PHOENIX.

THE GHOST:

Third Diary

"Did you know, the ghost roaming around in a house never realizes he is the ghost but wonders why you the strangers are roaming around his house?"

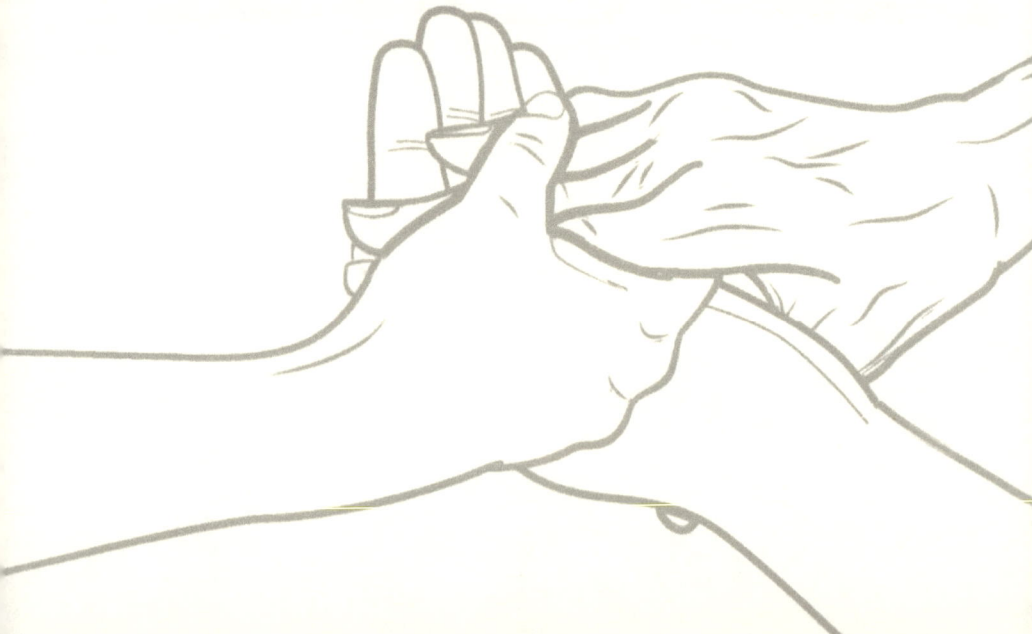

PROLOGUE:

Journey Back Home

"*Fear grips all until one is faced with the feared.*"

I am Aurelius van Phillip, and in this part, I will guide you all through the tunnel of light. I have traveled through this tunnel like a lot of you already have and more of you will in the future as we are all destined to this destiny. As I traveled through this tunnel, I got a chance to choose my life on Earth. I realized that's where I got confused and worried which path I should take.

It's terrifying and bewildering as I knew I was walking through the tunnel of death where everything suddenly became dark. Yet as I opened my eyes, there was light. There were so many different tunnels connecting to where I was. I just walked forward on to a bridge where I just wanted to go forward to my Creator. I heard someone call my name from behind me. I thought it was my adoptive mother Anadhi. She was crying and asking me to come back.

Memories from my life on Earth flooded my eyes as tears blocked my vision. I realized life was giving me another chance to prove my opinions, so I had to choose the right path. I wanted to journey back on to the path I had started a vision on. I wondered if Silas and Viviana were having a fair chance in life. I kept thinking about the two elderly people I had left behind. I wanted to be there with them when society was not. I wanted to be there to fight for them.

So, my journey through the tunnel of light was again a war between what was right and what was wrong. I wondered should I go back and help with the humanitarian crisis this world faced? With or without me, all will find their course. Should I reenter the world to finish the project I left behind? I wanted to finish this one project somehow some way. My Big Mama Anadhi had told me where there is hope, there is a way. I wanted to see her one more time and tell this world a mother is not just the person who gives birth but the person who is there for you throughout everything.

What would you do if you had a chance to reenter the world and have a second chance at life? Maybe this time, I won't fight to stay alive every day of my life. Maybe I could have a father's hand and a mother's blessings on my head as I travel through life once again. Let's travel through the tunnel of light back toward the door of reincarnation. All you must do is just believe in it. Come along and let's find out if I can journey back to where my heart beats were left behind on a journey back home.

JOURNEY BACK HOME

Birth and death

Are connected

Through

The journey

Of a person's lifetime.

Throughout the trip

On Earth,

You create

A story.

You bring into

This story

New people.

You make

A home

And at the

End of the day,

You wait for sunsets

To end the day,

However, some people

Return to the

End line

Before the sun sets

In their lives.

It's then

They

All over again,

Get back on

The path and

JOURNEY BACK HOME.

EPILOGUE:

The Bride, The Groom, And The Ghost

"The journey through life is a timeline. Do not accept a mindset but accept the changes. Who says you age with time, for I believe your biological clock sets to zero at the end as you awaken as a child again through reincarnation."

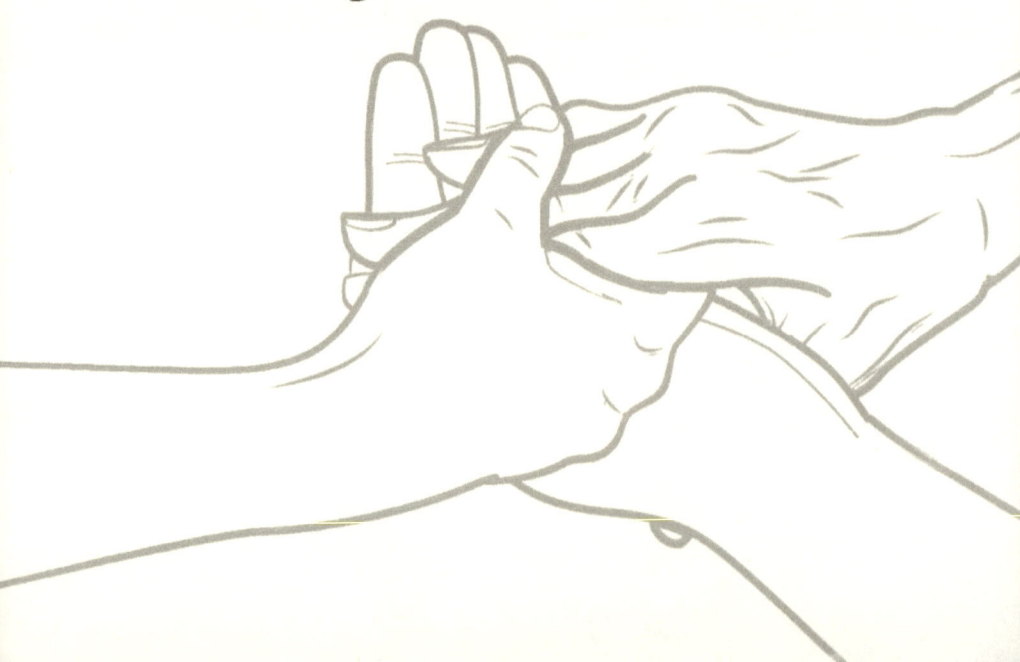

The journey through the tunnel of light was not as scary as I had feared. All right, I didn't tell any one of you, but I was scared. The journey was not fearful, yet fear gripped my inner soul thinking about what happens after death. I started to walk through the tunnel when I recalled my buddy Andries had told me not to be scared. Just walk through bravely. It's so confusing as there were so many doors. I knew I had to open the right one. I remembered Jacobus had told me to take the door of reincarnation.

I worried what happens to people who belong to no religious groups. I was an orphan who never belonged to any home of worshiping as I was never introduced to any. I grew up believing nothing existed. The Kasteel Vrederic family members believe in all religions as one. I too started to believe maybe I didn't belong to any house of worshipping but to my Creator. I am his as he created me too.

It was then I heard a voice. A very calming voice was reciting a poem, a prayer out to me. I knew the voice was trying to give me back my faith in my Creator. The calming voice recited the following words only to calm me at the time when I fought between life and death.

NEVER FEAR, FOR I AM HERE

When there is fear,

I am here.

When there are worries,

I shall make them disappear.

When there is nothing,

I shall give you something.

Never fear,

For I am here.

For where there is no one,

I am there.

When there is everyone,

I am still here.

When there is no one,

I am still here.

Never fear,

For I am here.

For even though

You close your eyes to me,

I never close my eyes on you.

When you lay in bed asleep,

I stay awake only to protect you.

For when dawn arrives,

I still am by your side,

And when dawn becomes dusk,

I still am here.

Never fear,

For I am here.

For from my breath,

You breathed.

From my hands,

You the human become.

With my will,

You became a man,

Yet with your will or without,

I am here.

Now get to know me,

I am your one and only Creator.

So today

I tell you,

Through life

And through death,

Through good,

And through bad,

NEVER FEAR, FOR I AM HERE.

As I listened to the prevailing words of my Creator, I knew he existed for even me, who never believed he existed. I felt like my Creator just gave me his warm comforting hugs. Even though life did not give me a chance to get to know him, he just told me he still knew me. My Creator knew I existed and am walking through the tunnel of death.

It mattered not I never worshipped any one God, my Creator walked by my side always. I felt like all the stories of God the Creator being only a judge like the Earthly courts was removed from my soul. As today my Creator told me not to fear anything as he is by my side. He was always there and shall always be there by my side, even when I am walking as a dead.

I know with the words of my Creator as my comfort and guide, I walked through the tunnel of light bravely as I kept on hearing his words of comfort to never fear. The tunnel was white and golden, and it seemed like the light makes everyone dizzy. There were different escalators and elevators connecting different tunnels.

I stood for a while as I called out for some help. I worried why the whole tunnel was empty if I knew there are people traveling on this route daily. I realized everyone was invisible to me as this was my journey. I could not follow anyone as I traveled alone. I knew even when there was no one in sight my Creator was there invisibly by my side.

There were a lot of doors in front of me. For some reason I could only read what was written on one door. A door in front of me was a little ajar as all the rest were closed. This door had a sign which read, "Rebirth." I knew I wanted a second chance in life, so I opened the door completely. There were pictures of humans I had known all over the walls, they were like television sets.

I saw families waiting for their child to come down to them. There were people praying for children. I walked past all these television sets. As I saw there was a woman sitting on a porch and a man was sitting next to her. They were both crying for some weird reason I wanted to find out more about this couple.

I pressed a button that read next. There I saw the porch and the house I had once bought and then Silas had bought, and now lives there with his wife Viviana. I walked closer to the screen and saw they were both crying.

There was a neighbor who had gifted them black balloons. The woman said, "These balloons represent elderly couples like yourselves. If you guys need any help walking or mowing or just need to call the ambulance, please ask for help."

The neighbor meant well but left my family crying. I saw Viviana ask Silas, "Are we too old to be married and wanting a love story for ourselves? Why is everyone questioning why we decided to marry at this age? We just finished a war with the dragon now. Every day we have someone or another asking or reminding us we are too old. I find my life with you is never a story that ends but only becomes eternal through our love."

Silas stood up and watched the great Mississippi River as he rubbed his cheeks, something he always had done. He brushed his hair and folded his fingers, then let go of them.

He laughed and said to his wife, "I fought my whole life trying to teach people golden age is not to be feared. Life does not stop at sixty, nor does it stop at twenty. For life is a gift. Live it with grace and blessings and don't fear the time left but enjoy the time you do have. We have today and this is now our eternal moment. Don't worry what others say or don't say, we live our life our own way and maybe we can teach everyone to have a broader mindset."

I realized they were still going through ageism. I wondered what about the beast? Is he reborn or he was burnt to ashes. Does everyone get a second chance or just hand-picked ones? The memories of fighting the wild beast still gave me the shivers which even death could not overtake.

The thunder was roaring as my two favorite people did not run inside. They laughed and were playing in the rain. I saw behind them was an animal running loose. I wondered was it a fox that was hiding behind the bushes? Then I saw there was a baby crocodile trying to get into the backyard. Somehow, it slid inside from the Mississippi River.

The crocodile was trying to break the steel iron fence with its head and slide in. I worried for the two people I had left behind and somehow knew they could take care of themselves, but I was the one who needed to be with them to make sure I could handle the separation. Some stories have three not two people and I knew this story was such a story.

I had found my family and my parents. I pressed the button as I wished to be born to this elderly couple. The journey would be hard, but I knew we could do it together. As they will be there for me, so shall I be there for them from anywhere and anyhow.

Ten months from that day, I opened my eyes in the Vrederic Hospital, the same hospital where I had taken my last breath in. Dr. Margriete and Dr. Jacobus were watching me. They both handed me over to Viviana my mother.

I heard my mother say, "No, let Anadhi have him as she is his godmother. Let her carry him first for it is her faith that brought him back to us. I am old and I need help from all of you. This is a miracle from beyond. How could I at sixty-two years of age have carried him?"

Anadhi came and kissed my cheeks as she said, "Welcome back home my godson."

That night, I went home with my parents and knew in this life I have the best parents ever. My Mama kept the windows open as Papa held on to me and my Mama. My mother then said no more ghosts my son for now. We are all Vivours. I am Viviana Stella Vivour, your Papa is Silas Coleridge Vivour, and you are Aurelius Coleridge Vivour."

I saw the Mississippi River and only wondered how does reincarnation work? The beast and I had fought in the river when I saw myself rise from the ashes. Yet I wonder did he the dragon too rise again or is he gone forever? In any case, I will be here protecting my parents if he does decide to rise again. Maybe I won't have the tears of the magical phoenix to defeat him, but I will defeat him through love I have for my family. Life is a circle and at times, these circles are completed through reincarnation.

Mr. Drake Crow, the demon in this life is my biological grandfather as he had sired my father through his mistress. The mysteries behind my birth and rebirth were due to my biological racist grandfather. A black man was reincarnated as a white man as he was sired by his past-life racist murderer who even preferred a white mistress. Yet little did the murderer know, his white son would sire me, his worst enemy.

Within my biological father, still was intact his past-life soul. The skin color never changed the soul. Today, I too have traveled through the door of death to defeat and avenge a racist only by being born from his own bloodline. I have been reborn all because of him, through his lineage. My birth proves where there is a demon, there is an angel who too shall rise and die to be reborn again, only to prove that at the end, truth and just shall always triumph, even when the war is happening in the same family.

Today, we are a family living happily in New Orleans, Louisiana. I remember how we had united in this same house, as even now people whisper there once was a roaring dragon behind that house. People still talk about the mysterious diary that was written through magical ink and had written a story on its own. This famous story related to the house by the Mississippi River, is famously called, *The Bride, The Groom, And The Ghost.*

THE BRIDE, THE GROOM, AND THE GHOST

The world watches a family,

Growing old together,

Yet a family grows young together,

As a son is welcomed

Back from

The beyond.

For not

All families

Are alike

As all

Fingers

Are different.

In one hand,

The families too

Come in different

Ways.

Some are adopted.

Some are biological.

Some are brought

Together

Through obstacles.

Yet soul families

Who end up

Together are

Meant to be together

Through

Time

After time,

As we

Are

A family

Formed originally

By,

THE BRIDE, THE GROOM, AND THE GHOST.

DWELLERS WITHIN THE BRIDE, THE GROOM, AND THE GHOST

Viviana Stella (Froster) Vivour   Bride, wife, and twin flame of Silas Coleridge Vivour, traveling as the ghost bride since her murder in 1866.

Silas Coleridge Vivour   Black freedman murdered in 1866, reborn in the twentieth century as the white illegitimate son of Drake Crow. Groom, husband, and twin flame of Viviana Stella (Froster) Vivour.

Aurelius van Phillip/Aurelius Coleridge Vivour   Orphan adopted by Erasmus van Phillip and Anadhi Newhouse van Philip, reborn to Viviana Stella (Froster) Vivour and Silas Coleridge Vivour.

Drake Crow   Racist businessman and murderer in the nineteenth century, reborn as the biological father of Silas Coleridge Vivour in the twentieth century. After death, incarnated as the demon residing below the Mississippi River.

Andrew Froster   White nationalist and brother of Viviana Stella (Froster) Vivour in the nineteenth century.

234

SPECIAL APPEARANCES FROM THE *KASTEEL VREDERIC* SERIES

Erasmus van Phillip World-renowned painter, and twenty-first-century owner of Kasteel Vrederic. Son of Greta van Phillip, descendant of the van Vrederic family, twin flame and husband of Anadhi Newhouse van Phillip, father of Dr. Jacobus Vrederic van Phillip, uncle and adoptive father of Antonius van Phillip and Andries van Phillip, and grandfather of reincarnated Andries van Phillip, Griet Vrederic van Phillip, and Rietje Vrederic van Phillip. Reincarnated form of sixteenth-century Johannes van Vrederic.

Anadhi Newhouse van Phillip Author. Daughter of Dr. Andrew Newhouse and Dr. Gita Shankar Newhouse, granddaughter of Martin Newhouse and Miranda Newhouse, granddaughter of Hari Shankar and Parvati Shankar, twin flame and wife of Erasmus van Phillip, mother of Dr. Jacobus Vrederic van Phillip, aunt and adoptive mother of Antonius van Phillip and Andries van Phillip, grandmother of

235

reincarnated Andries van Phillip, Griet Vrederic van Phillip, and Rietje Vrederic van Phillip. Reincarnated form of sixteenth-century Mahalt.

Dr. Jacobus Vrederic van Phillip
Medical doctor with multiple specialties, and one-of-a-kind specialist in never-done-before transplant surgeries. Son of Erasmus van Phillip and Anadhi Newhouse van Phillip, cousin of Antonius van Phillip and Andries van Phillip, uncle of reincarnated Andries van Phillip and Griet Vrederic van Phillip, twin flame and husband of Dr. Margriete van Achthoven van Phillip, and father of Rietje Vrederic van Phillip. Reincarnated form of sixteenth and seventeenth-century Jacobus van Vrederic.

Antonius van Phillip
World-renowned painter. Son of Petrus van Phillip and Giada Berlusconi van Phillip, nephew and adopted son of Erasmus van Phillip and Anadhi Newhouse van Phillip, twin brother of Andries van Phillip, cousin and adoptive brother of Dr. Jacobus Vrederic van Phillip, twin flame and husband of Katelijne Snaaijer van Phillip, and father of

reincarnated Andries van Phillip and Griet Vrederic van Phillip.

Andries van Phillip   Deceased world-renowned pianist, son of Petrus van Phillip and Giada Berlusconi van Phillip, nephew and adopted son of Erasmus van Phillip and Anadhi Newhouse van Phillip, twin brother of Antonius van Phillip, and cousin and adoptive brother of Dr. Jacobus Vrederic van Phillip. Now reincarnated son of Antonius van Phillip and Katelijne Snaaijer van Phillip, grandson of Erasmus van Phillip and Anadhi Newhouse van Phillip, nephew of Dr. Jacobus Vrederic van Phillip and Dr. Margriete van Achthoven van Phillip, brother of Griet Vrederic van Phillip, cousin of Rietje Vrederic van Phillip, twin flame and husband of Tara Bella, and adoptive father of Hana Bella van Phillip and Ahana Bella van Phillip.

Agatha Newhouse Brown "Aunt Agatha"   Twin flame and wife of James Brown. Nurse and former nun, grandaunt of Anadhi Newhouse van Phillip, and descendant of the family of Aunt Marinda.

James Brown "Uncle James"   Twin flame and husband of Agatha Newhouse Brown.

Dreamer, seeker, dream psychic, and preacher.

Aunt Marinda — Time traveler, spiritual seer, nurse, and herbalist from the sixteenth century in the present day. Co-owner of Agatha and Marinda's Orphanage. Sister of Agatha and Tabitha, adoptive guardian of Theunis and Alexander, and twin flame and wife of Kees van Vrederic.

Dr. Margriete van Achthoven van Phillip — Medical doctor, cardiologist, and pediatric cardiovascular surgeon. Co-owner of Agatha and Marinda's Orphanage. Twin flame and wife of Dr. Jacobus Vrederic van Phillip, and mother of Rietje Vrederic van Phillip. Reincarnated form of sixteenth and seventeenth-century Margriete van Wijck.

Katelijne Snaaijer van Phillip — Stepdaughter of Ghileyn Snaaijer, twin flame and wife of Antonius van Phillip, and mother of reincarnated Andries van Phillip and Griet Vrederic van Phillip.

Tara Bella van Phillip — Daughter of Sitara Bella and Marcello Esposito, twin flame and wife of Andries van Phillip, and adoptive mother of Hana Bella van Phillip and Ahana Bella van Phillip.

Griet Vrederic van Phillip Daughter of Sitara Bella and Marcello Esposito, twin flame and wife of Andries van Phillip, and adoptive mother of Hana Bella van Phillip and Ahana Bella van Phillip.

Rietje Vrederic van Phillip Daughter of Dr. Jacobus Vrederic van Phillip and Dr. Margriete van Achthoven van Phillip, granddaughter of Erasmus van Phillip and Anadhi Newhouse van Phillip, and cousin of Andries van Phillip and Griet Vrederic van Phillip. Reincarnated form of sixteenth and seventeenth-century Margriete "Rietje" Jacobus Peters.

Theunis Peters Adopted son of Aunt Marinda. Adoptive brother of Alexander. Reincarnated form of sixteenth-century Theunis Peters.

Alexander van der Bijl Adopted son of Aunt Marinda. Adoptive brother of Theunis. Reincarnated form of sixteenth and seventeenth-century Sir Alexander van der Bijl. Cousin of seventeenth-century Frederic van der Bijl.

Ahana Roy Child bride, and birth mother of Hana Bella van Phillip and Ahana Bella van Phillip. Reincarnated form of seventeenth-century

Ahana and twin flame of Frederic van der Bijl.

Ahana Bella van Phillip   Biological daughter of Ahana Roy and adopted daughter of Andries van Phillip and Tara Bella van Phillip.

Hana Bella van Phillip   Biological daughter of Ahana Roy and adopted daughter of Andries van Phillip and Tara Bella van Phillip.

GLOSSARY

Get acquainted with some terms and places that were used in this book.

1866 New Orleans Massacre On July 30, 1866, a group of white rioters brutally attacked and massacred black freedmen who were marching for their voting rights.

US Abolition of Slavery The thirteenth amendment of the US Constitution in December 1865 abolished slavery in the United States.

Ageism Discrimination against an individual based on age.

Algiers Point Second-oldest neighborhood of New Orleans established in 1719 by the French along the Mississippi River across from the French Quarter.

Amsterdam Capital city of the Netherlands.

Andrew Jackson Seventh President of the United States who is remembered for his pro-slavery and anti-Native American stances.

Beignet Deep fried square pastries.

Bourbon Street Historic road that stretches thirteen blocks through the French Quarter.

Café Du Monde Café that has been selling beignets and café au lait in the French Quarter since 1862.

Confederate States of America Initially consisted of seven pro-slavery states, and later eleven, from 1861 to 1865 including Louisiana.

Dream Psychic One who sees past, present, and future through dreams.

Egypt Country in Northern Africa.

England Country in Europe.

Evermore Beloved Garden Family graveyard in the *Kasteel Vrederic* series.

French Quarter Oldest neighborhood in New Orleans established in 1718 by the French along the Mississippi River.

Ghost A soul that is not contained within a physical body.

Gulf of Mexico The Mississippi River drains into the Gulf of Mexico at the Mississippi River Delta in Louisiana.

Hurricane Katrina   Category 5 hurricane that caused massive destruction and deaths especially in New Orleans where levees failed to keep flood waters out.

Immunocompromised   An individual whose immune system is weakened or impaired.

Kasteel Vrederic   Castle Vrederic which was made for the *Kasteel Vrederic* book series is home to a time-traveling paranormal family.

Louisiana   The 18th state of the United States located off the Gulf of Mexico.

Mardi Gras   Celebration before Ash Wednesday and Lent.

Masoor Dal   Red lentils.

Mississippi River   River that goes across ten states in the United States.

Naarden   City in the Netherlands, home of the Kasteel Vrederic family.

Napoleon Bonaparte   French emperor who sold the Louisiana territory to the United States in 1803.

New Orleans City and parish along the Mississippi River in Louisiana, nicknamed "The Big Easy."

New York City City located in the state of New York, known as the "Big Apple."

Phoenix Mythical bird that burns but rises again from ashes.

Reincarnation Belief system of a lot of people worldwide such as Buddhism, Hinduism, Jainism, Sikhism, and more. Today science can't disprove reincarnation. Also a lot of people have given proof of their rebirth. More information on reincarnation can be found in the book *Eternal Truth: The Tunnel Of Light* by Ann Marie Ruby.

Tennessee State in southeastern United States.

The Netherlands Country in Western Europe.

Tunnel Of Light Scientifically it is known as the NDE (near-death experience) tunnel. More information on the tunnel of light can be found in the book *Eternal Truth: The Tunnel Of Light* by Ann Marie Ruby.

Twin Flames   Research has shown twin
flames can survive as
individuals yet are complete as
one. More information on twin
flames can be found in the
book *Eternal Truth: The
Tunnel Of Light* by Ann Marie
Ruby.

MESSAGE FROM THE AUTHOR

"When hate is thrown
into the air, the wind it
produces will come and
touch you, as the air
only circulates back,
just like discrimination
is an act of the
discriminators, waiting
to be circulated back to
its creators."

Ageism is a stigma directed toward the elderly population. This stigma increases its vital scrutiny when people hear the word immunocompromised. The discriminatory treatment these people receive has no boundary. This treatment is also given to the young generations who are too young or not experienced enough. If an individual has any form of physical disabilities, then the young and the old fall into the same boat and face discrimination.

I had to do something about these issues. I placed this humanitarian crisis into the paranormal gothic world of Kasteel Vrederic where I could solve the issues through miracles from the beyond. As you too are now aware of how big this issue is, then you too could do something about this at your workplaces. If you see a person being unjustly terminated from his or her job because of ageism, speak out. Think about Aurelius, Silas, and all of those who don't have a voice, yet you do.

The elderly people who are waiting outside to get into the hotels or places of worship or just want to enjoy dinner at times are not accommodated. As all available seats are after they please the young and fit, most places have limited spaces to maneuver around. I connected ageism to health issues as I am diabetic. I found this out as it's at times hard to go out to dinner or different workplaces or hotels who have all-inclusive meals as they are not diabetic friendly.

I also have on several occasions had to prove to many why I must limit my intake of carbohydrates. It's not a fashion statement but a way for diabetics to survive normally. Yet every point of my life I find I must make a point and must prove myself why I can't have carbohydrates rather than others trying to understand why diabetics avoid carbohydrates. For some, it's not a fashion statement but survival. Humans at times become the biggest critics of humans. Yet never think you too might end up on the same stage today you criticize.

Science has moved forward. It is helping people live longer and healthier lives. Yet we the people of this society have left out the acceptance of science behind with our unacceptable behaviors toward the elderly, the immunocompromised, the young, and those who can't speak for themselves. Think how easy it was for you to just put someone down, yet now could you go back in time and take back your unjust painful words.

Discrimination against race, color, and religious beliefs has been around and at times people just try to accommodate the divider rather than accommodate the person left behind. These behavioral traits have now touched our elderly population who at times are immunocompromised.

I have written this book to awaken the society members who have left behind our elders, our youngsters, and the immunocompromised. I feel like all three groups of people are excluded from the society as people fear them. Fear is the divider as individuals have inferiority complexes in fear and will not acknowledge this as a trait.

Death is near when you are old, so people fear the old as they fear death. The young people feel excluded and at times are made to feel they are inexperienced. The older generations are afraid of the young and their newly acquired knowledge. The immunocompromised group is feared as people don't want to be sick or around them again in fear of the unknown diseases they might carry.

As discrimination is the problem for all these issues, the answer to all these problems is hidden within knowledge. My message is don't fear the unknown but fear the lack of knowledge.

Gain knowledge on all these topics. See through the eyes of the elderly, through the eyes of the young, and through the eyes of the sick. Maybe spend a day with them. Walk with them and try to see through their eyes.

Feel for them as you feel for your own self. It's hard to feel the pain of the strangers who have an open wound as you will at times try to put a bandage on it for them or maybe because then you won't have to see their wounds. At times you will walk away in fear of getting sick for how could you feel the migraine pain of the person standing next to you if you have never had one?

You have just read this gothic tale, where I can change the fate of my characters through the power of my pen. Unlike in this unjust world, I cannot be there with the people who have gone through these discriminatory practices. Maybe as you fall in love with Silas, Aurelius, and Viviana, through them I can make you love the elderly like you would love Silas.

Maybe you would look at the sick differently as you learn to love Aurelius. Also don't fear the end of life as that's just part of the journey. Don't fear patients who have been asleep for years and are trying to get back into the society they had left behind or have moved on forward without them. Don't fear ghosts you might encounter as you walk through graveyards or maybe centuries-old manor houses for the ghosts you fear tonight once walked by your side.

I know the child born today will be a hundred years old just a hundred years from today. So, it's your journey to be the elderly tomorrow. Treat the elders like you want to be treated tomorrow. You were the young yesterday so treat the young generations like you wanted to be treated but were not yesterday. The sick and immunocompromised people walking next to you, don't ignore them. Remember the times you were sick and there was no one by your side who could have brought you a simple cup of tea. Be the person who treats all with a warm cup of tea. Be there for others even if they were never there for you. Teach all with kindness, not anger and revenge.

If today at your work, school, worshipping place, or just in a hotel, you see a person discriminating against anyone for any reason that falls into hate or discriminatory practices, speak up. Don't look the other way because it's not your problem today. Remember life is a wagon of karma. You never know when you too will be walking on the same path as the one you ignored or did not stand up for.

Yet if we all stand up against ageism and all discriminatory practices today, in the future as we become the elderly or suffer from any of these obstacles, there will be all of us protecting one another. All discriminatory practitioners will be extinct as we the humans all learn to love Silas, Aurelius, and Viviana.

The reason I placed my characters in a gothic thriller is to make sure you too see them as your beloved characters who suffered through ageism, racial, physical, and all other discriminations.

Learn to love all as then you too will be loved. As you walk upon the path of these discriminatory practitioners, you and I together will say no to all types of discrimination as it's going against Silas, Aurelius, and Viviana.

In all my books, I talk about death as I believe life on Earth is but a day. My message to all of you is don't fear the end as it is always there. Life is a journey where some leave us before we are ready to let them go; however, they are getting ready to be reborn or maybe will meet their Creator. This journey we will all have to take at the end of our journey through life.

Maybe you too will hear the poem Aurelius heard as he was traveling through the tunnel of light. For then you will believe there is no fear for whatever you believe our Creator always watches over us. Let's not fear the end but may all have faith in a new beginning. Enjoy life and don't fear death.

Also, for as long as we are on Earth, let's see one another as a human friend and a human family member. Be a humanitarian and know someone out there is watching out for you too. It matters not if your hands are withered like Silas or see-through like Viviana the dream traveler or ghostly dead and cold like Aurelius's. Let's give everyone our helping hands. For amongst all humans across this globe tonight walks my gothic paranormal family, the bride, the groom, and the ghost.

ABOUT THE AUTHOR

"Meet Ann Marie Ruby from California.
This is her story."

Ann Marie Ruby was born into a diplomatic family for which she had the privilege of traveling the world. This upbringing made the whole world her one family. She never saw a country as a foreign country yet as a neighbor who was there for her as she would be there for them. After all, isn't that what families do for one another?

Ann Marie became an author as she started to place her chosen words into the pages of her diaries. She knew she must collect all her thoughts and produce them into different diaries. Each diary became her different books.

Ann Marie's life goal is not to just write something but only what she believes in. So all her thoughts and words remained within the pages of her diaries until she realized it was time she must share them with you. Otherwise, she felt selfish and knew that was not her characteristic as she lives for everyone, not just for herself.

INTERNATIONAL #1 BESTSELLING AUTHOR:

Ann Marie became an international number-one bestselling author of twenty-four books. Alongside being a full-time author. She loves to write articles on her website where she can have a better connection with all of you. Ann Marie, a dream psychic, became a blogger and a humanitarian only because she believes in you and herself as a complete, honest, and open family.

PERSONAL:

Ann Marie is an American who grew up in Brisbane, Australia. She resided in the Washington, D.C. area, later settled in Seattle, Washington, and currently lives in California. In her spare time when she is not writing books, she loves to meditate, pray, listen to music, cook, and write blog posts.

BESTSELLING:

Ann Marie's books have placed her on top 100 bestselling charts in various countries including the Netherlands, United States, United Kingdom, Canada, and Germany. In 2020, she became a household name as her books began to consistently rank #1 on multiple bestselling charts. *The Netherlands: Land Of My Dreams* and *Everblooming: Through The Twelve Provinces Of The Netherlands*, both became overnight number-one bestsellers in the United States.

In 2020, *The Netherlands: Land Of My Dreams* also became a bestseller in the Netherlands and Canada, consistently becoming #1 on various lists and one of the top selling books on Amazon NL. *Everblooming: Through The Twelve Provinces Of The Netherlands* became #37 on the Netherlands top 100 bestselling Amazon books chart which includes all books from all genres. Ann Marie's other books have also made various top 100 bestselling lists and received multiple accolades including *Eternal Truth: The Tunnel Of Light* which was named as one of eight thought-provoking books by women.

ROMANCE FICTION:

Ann Marie's *Kasteel Vrederic* series was written in a diary fashion. She has always kept a diary herself, so she thought her characters too could keep a diary. All of their diaries became individual books yet collectively, they are a part of a family, the Kasteel Vrederic family.

OTHER BOOKS:

All of Ann Marie's nonfiction and fiction books are available globally. You can take a look at short descriptions about the books at the end of this book.

THE NETHERLANDS:

Ann Marie revealed why many of her books revolve around the Netherlands, sharing that as a dream psychic, she had seen the historical past of a country in her dreams and was later able to place a name to the country. This is described in detail in *Spiritual Lighthouse: The Dream Diaries Of Ann Marie Ruby* and *The Netherlands: Land Of My Dreams* where she also wrote about her plans to eventually move to the Netherlands.

Ann Marie has received letters on behalf of His Majesty King Willem-Alexander and Her Majesty Queen Máxima of the Netherlands after they received her books *The Netherlands: Land Of My Dreams* and *Everblooming: Through The Twelve Provinces Of The Netherlands*. Additionally, Ann Marie has received letters on behalf of His Excellency Mark Rutte, the Prime Minister of the Netherlands for her books.

WRITING:

Ann Marie also is acclaimed globally as one of the top voices in the spiritual space, however, she is recognized for her writing abilities published across many genres namely spirituality, lifestyle, inspirational quotations, poetry, fiction, romance, history, travel, social awareness, and more. Her writing style is hailed by critics and readers alike as making readers feel as though they have made a friend.

FOLLOW THE AUTHOR:

Now as you have found her book, why don't you and Ann Marie become friends? Join her and become a part of her global family. Ann Marie shall always give you books which you will read and then find yourself as a part of her book family.

For more information about Ann Marie Ruby, any one of her books, or to read her blog posts and articles, subscribe to her website, www.annmarieruby.com.

Follow Ann Marie Ruby on Twitter, Facebook, Instagram, Threads, and Pinterest:

@TheAnnMarieRuby

BOOKS BY THE AUTHOR

INSPIRATIONAL QUOTATIONS SERIES:

This series includes four books of original quotations and one omnibus edition.

Spiritual Travelers:
Life's Journey From The Past
To The Present
For The Future

Spiritual
Messages:
From A Bottle

Spiritual Journey:
Life's Eternal Blessings

Spiritual
Inspirations:
Sacred Words
Of Wisdom

Omnibus edition contains all four books of original quotations.

Spiritual Ark:
The Enchanted Journey Of Timeless
Quotations

SPIRITUAL SONGS **SERIES:**

This series includes two original spiritual prayer books.

SPIRITUAL SONGS: LETTERS FROM MY CHEST

When there was no hope, I found hope within these sacred words of prayers, I but call songs. Within this book, I have for you, 100 very sacred prayers.

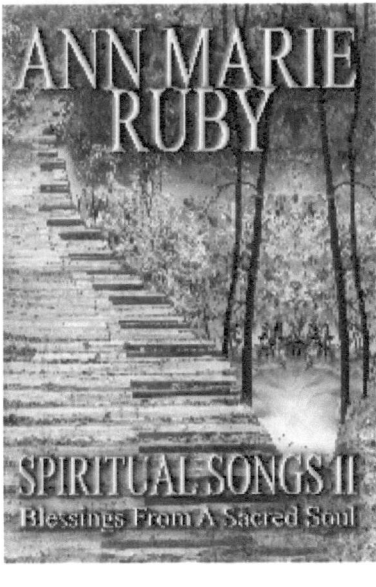

SPIRITUAL SONGS II: BLESSINGS FROM A SACRED SOUL

Prayers are but the sacred doors to an individual's enlightenment. This book has 123 prayers for all humans with humanity.

SPIRITUAL LIGHTHOUSE: THE DREAM DIARIES OF ANN MARIE RUBY

Do you believe in dreams? For within each individual dream, there is a hidden message and a miracle interlinked. Learn the spiritual, scientific, religious, and philosophical aspects of dreams. Walk with me as you travel through forty nights, through the pages of my book.

THE WORLD HATE CRISIS: THROUGH THE EYES OF A DREAM PSYCHIC

Humans have walked into an age where humanity now is being questioned as hate crimes have reached a catastrophic amount. Let us in union stop this crisis. Pick up my book and see if you too could join me in this fight.

ETERNAL TRUTH: THE TUNNEL OF LIGHT

Within this book, travel with me through the doors of birth, death, reincarnation, true soulmates and twin flames, dreams, miracles, and the end of time.

THE NETHERLANDS: LAND OF MY DREAMS

Oh the sacred travelers, be like the mystical river and journey through this blessed land through my book. Be the flying bird of wisdom and learn about a land I call, Heaven on Earth.

EVERBLOOMING: THROUGH THE TWELVE PROVINCES OF THE NETHERLANDS

Original poetry and hand-picked tales are bound together in this keepsake book. Come travel with me as I take you through the lives of the Dutch past.

LOVE LETTERS: THE TIMELESS TREASURE

Fifty original timeless treasured love poems are presented with individual illustrations describing each poem.

MELODIES OF HUMANITY: THE GOLDEN KEYS

Thirty-two poems retell the melodies of humanity, calling all humans to awaken their humanity through love, the golden keys everyone carries within their inner souls.

KASTEEL VREDERIC SERIES:

ETERNALLY BELOVED: I SHALL NEVER LET YOU GO

Travel time to the sixteenth century where Jacobus van Vrederic, a beloved lover and father, surmounts time and tide to find the vanished love of his life. On his pursuit, Jacobus discovers secrets that will alter his life evermore. He travels through the Eighty Years' War-ravaged country, the Netherlands as he takes the vow, even if separated by a breath, "Eternally beloved, I shall never let you go."

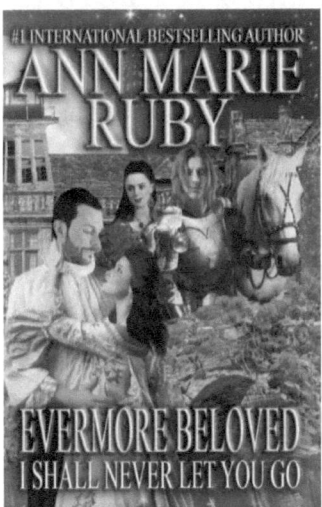

EVERMORE BELOVED: I SHALL NEVER LET YOU GO

Jacobus van Vrederic returns with the devoted spirits of Kasteel Vrederic. A knight and a seer also join him on a quest to find his lost evermore beloved. They journey through a war-ravaged country, the Netherlands, to stop another war which was brewing silently in his land, called the witch hunts. Time was his enemy as he must defeat time and tide to find his evermore beloved wife alive.

BE MY DESTINY: VOWS FROM THE BEYOND

Fighting their biggest enemy destiny, twin flames Erasmus van Phillip and Anadhi Newhouse are reborn over and over again only to lose the battle to destiny. Find out if through the helping hands of sacred spirits of the sixteenth century, these eternal twin flames are finally able to unite in the twenty-first century, as they say, "Reincarnation is a blessing if only you are mine."

HEART BEATS YOUR NAME: VOWS FROM THE BEYOND

While one is sleepless, the other twin flame is sleeping eternally. Now how does Antonius van Phillip awaken his twin flame Katelijne Snaaijer from beyond Earth, and solve a murder mystery, she is the only witness to yet also a victim of? Find out how the musical sound of heartbeats guide him to his sleeping beloved while he solves the mystery sleepless.

ENTRANCED BELOVED: I SHALL NEVER LET YOU GO

The pages of Margriete "Rietje" Jacobus Peters's love story from her diary slowly go missing from the library of Kasteel Vrederic. The twenty-first-century descendants fighting death and time must travel back in time to save their ancestors and their beloved Kasteel Vrederic. Traveling through the tunnel of light, the family of the twenty-first century must save the seventeenth-century twin flames. Rietje and her beloved twin flame Sir Alexander van der Bijl must create another paranormal, magical, historical, romantic diary for the dynasty to even exist.

FORBIDDEN DAUGHTER OF KASTEEL VREDERIC: VOWS FROM THE BEYOND

Jacobus Vrederic van Phillip stopped pouring tears and burning himself with memories of passion to become a stone, so he could live with memories and not recreate new ones. The Vrederic family members realize the curse of past life's karma will come and meet them in this life and erase the only child who kept the dynasty going, the child known to all as the forbidden daughter of Kasteel Vrederic. The man who has sacrificed his life for all members of his family and society now must find a way to awaken his sleeping soul, recognize his twin flame, and bring back as the beloved daughter the only child he had rejected. To this world she was known as the forbidden daughter of Kasteel Vrederic.

THE IMMORTALITY SERUM: VOWS FROM THE BEYOND

Andries van Phillip, the famous pianist, gets calls from his dead twin flame Tara Bella in his dreams. All dressed in red, she roams around a burning castle trying to rescue all the people from within, without realizing she was the victim, not Andries. Now the paranormal family travels across the ocean as they fight Succubus the demoness, rescue the woman in red, and solve a murder mystery, all while they know before time ends, they must find the immortality serum.

Coming Soon

WOMAN IN THE MIRROR: VOWS FROM THE BEYOND

WOMAN IN THE MIRROR: VOWS FROM THE BEYOND

The eighth book in this series is coming soon.

Coming Soon

BRIDE OF THE IMMORTAL: VOWS FROM THE BEYOND

BRIDE OF THE IMMORTAL: VOWS FROM THE BEYOND

The ninth book in this series is coming soon.

#1 INTERNATIONAL BESTSELLING AUTHOR
ANN MARIE RUBY

SHATTERED WINGS
DIARY OF A CHILD BRIDE

SHATTERED WINGS: DIARY OF A CHILD BRIDE

Ahana Roy fought this unkind world to make room for her in this society, where she would not go to bed hungry. She was brought to the city of dreams where her dreams were shattered as she became a child bride. How will she fight the war of being a child bride in a city that has no idea of her existence? In her shattered dreams, she found a ghost sailor who promised to be with her, dead or alive. Following the advice of a dead sailor, Ahana wandered the streets of New York City looking for help. There she found the paranormal family of Kasteel Vrederic as her helping hands. This is the diary of child bride who said, "I had no chance in life as I was born with shattered wings."

THE BRIDE, THE GROOM, AND THE GHOST

Viviana Stella Vivour was separated from her beloved groom during the 1866 massacre in New Orleans, Louisiana. For over a century, she has been roaming the streets of "The Big Easy" as a ghost bride. Now in the twenty-first century, Viviana's spirit is transported to her reincarnated past-life groom Silas Coleridge Vivour's historic Victorian home by the Mississippi River. She is shattered to witness him facing forced retirement through ageism. Separated by a breath, Viviana and Silas come face-to-face with their past-life enemy who became a demon to separate them again. The twin flames find solace in ways they never expected as there appears Aurelius van Phillip, a mysterious young man, who can see Viviana and the demon.

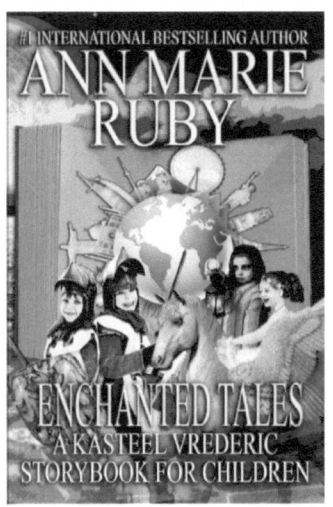

ENCHANTED TALES: A KASTEEL VREDERIC STORYBOOK FOR CHILDREN

Travel around the world in seven nights. Through enchanted tales you will meet and assist superheroes from the seven continents of this world. While there, you will learn about different cultures and landmarks. Keep your magical lanterns glowing as you help the girl with the lantern solve mysteries around the globe.

Coming Soon

BROTHER BEAR AND THE FOUR INVESTIGATORS: A KASTEEL VREDERIC STORYBOOK FOR CHILDREN

BROTHER BEAR AND THE FOUR INVESTIGATORS: A KASTEEL VREDERIC STORYBOOK FOR CHILDREN

Kasteel Vrederic's second storybook is coming soon.

www.ingramcontent.com/pod-product-compliance
Lightning Source LLC
Chambersburg PA
CBHW021510240626
47154CB00002B/575